Beauty and the Beast

Cover art by Mechelle Cotant

http://www.portraitsbymechelle.webs.com

Acknowledgements

This book has been a labor of love for many years, and many different people have helped me along while it has gone through different incarnations. I'd like to thank Cindy Krauchi, the best teacher I've ever had. Thanks to CoCo Hightshue, for giving her face to my Beauty. Thanks to my supportive friends Aimee, Lora, Dee, and Ginger. Thanks to my mom for proof-reading. And finally, thank you to my husband Michael and our children, Wolfgang, Cecily, and Westley. You make me happy.

Cecile reined in the heavy workhorse and turned back to survey the small plot of land she had just plowed. The rows were not quite perfectly straight, but she was doing much better than when she first learned this bit of farming. Since their move from the city, this acre garden was what kept them fed.

Her older sister Marie ran out of the cottage and stood with her hands on her hips and whined, "Father, look at her: straddling that horse like any common peasant. Tell her to act properly!"

Fabre sighed and called his youngest daughter back in from the garden. As she rode in, he shook his head in exasperation. "Cecile, please get down from there."

She swung her legs over the workhorse and jumped down. "What is it, Father?"

"Father wants you to act more like a lady and less like the stupid peasant girl that you are!" Marie snapped.

"Marie-Elise, please!" Fabre said patiently. "Cecile, we would appreciate it if you would act a little more properly."

The young woman pushed her tangled copper curls out of her eyes and said, "Father, I do quite a lot of work around here, and if I had to worry about being 'proper', I'd never get anything done. Now when you were a merchant and we lived in the city, I was very lady-like. But now we are peasants, and I see no reason to pretend otherwise."

Fabre nodded slowly, then turned to Marie and shrugged. "She does get a lot accomplished here."

Marie pouted and folded her arms. "Well, I don't care how poor we are, I'll never be a peasant!" she shouted, then burst into tears and ran into the cottage.

"I didn't mean to upset her, Father," Cecile said, looking after her sister.

"I know. She and Josette are just taking this a little harder than the rest of you. Be patient with them."

"Of course." She sighed and wiped the perspiration from her forehead with the corner of her apron, thinking that they had all been quite patient for over a year now. She had learned how to plow the field, grow vegetables, cook, milk the cow, and rick firewood, while her sisters occasionally made their bed.

"Well, I need to water Benjamin," she said, rubbing the horse's soft nose. "He's worked hard today."

Fabre kissed the top of her head. "You've worked about as hard as the horse. Why don't you rest for a little while?"

"I can't. I promised to help Victor and Gerard with the firewood."

"Let them get Edmond to help. Your brothers are old enough to take care of themselves. You rest."

"All right. But just for a little while. Then I'll start supper. Please ask Josette and Marie to set the table." It was a futile request, and she knew it, but she always asked.

"I'll tell them."

Cecile started back to their small barn, grateful for the chance to rest. In truth, she sometimes hated all of the work that their small farm required and wished that they were back in the city. In the last year, she had come to appreciate all of the work that their servants had done in taking care of them and wished that they still had those servants. Plowing and cleaning were things she detested. But her sisters complained so much that she felt there wasn't room for her grumbling, so she tried to cheerfully do as much as she could so at least her brothers wouldn't complain as well. None of them were used to much work, but they were all willing to learn. Her sisters, however, wailed for their city life whenever any work was asked of them, so their father would usually quietly ask Cecile to do whatever they had refused.

Once Benjamin was unharnessed and cared for, she walked into the cottage and lay down with one of the few books she was able to bring with her from their house in the city. When her father was a merchant, she had many books and loved them all; but within the space of one short year, they had lost their money through bad investments, several lost ships full of goods, and a warehouse fire. They were left with only enough money to retire to this small piece of property they owned in the country.

Cecile read a couple of pages of her beloved book, then, feeling rested, set about preparing supper. The meal that once consisted of rich foods such as pheasant, thick puddings, candied fruits, and wine was now generally a few potatoes, fish, bread, cheese, and milk. Cecile tried to add something special to their meager fare as often as she could; gathering berries for dessert, and learning how to make butter and jellies.

As she set the table—which neither Josette nor Marie could find the strength to do—she heard the sound of the quick pounding of horse's hooves. She ran outside to see what was happening, for it was not often that they had visitors so far out into the country.

The rest of the family had heard it as well and all had dropped what they were doing to see where the horse might be going. Cecile looked at them and laughed to herself. Once they had gone to the opera and the theatre for entertainment, and now they were all staring at a horse and rider pass their house.

But the rider did not pass them by. Instead, he reined in and leaped from his horse. "Are you the merchant Fabre?"

The old man walked out to meet the rider. "Yes, I am. What can we do for you?"

"Well now," the messenger said, brushing the dust off of his clothing, "I think it is what I can do for you."

Cecile quickly filled a cup with water and handed it to the young man. "What do you mean?"

"Thank you, mam'selle," he said as he took the offered cup. "I mean that I bring you news of one of your ships."

"But I haven't any more ships," Fabre said, confused.

"You have one. She made it into port last week. Damaged, but still afloat! And you are required in the city to deal with the cargo and the ship."

Fabre's face lit up. "Well," he said, "thank you for bringing us such good news! I'll return to the city tomorrow."

The messenger bowed as Fabre turned and walked back into the cottage, flanked by his children. All were talking excitedly about the possibility that with this ship, their fortune had been regained. All but Cecile, who stayed behind with the young man.

She followed him to his horse and asked frankly, "How badly is the ship actually damaged?"

He looked at her and shook his head. "There appears to be some that is salvageable, but it was a very bad storm that caught this ship."

"Will any money come of it?"

"Some, I'm sure."

"But not as much as my father is expecting."

"I'm sorry." He handed the cup back to her, and then climbed back onto his horse.

"There is a water trough at the barn, should your horse need it," she said, looking away from him.

He nodded. "Thank you."

"Do you require payment for your services?"

The young man scrutinized her closely, looking from her rough clothing to the smear of flour across her cheek, and gave her a sympathetic smile. "That isn't necessary. Those who sent me will pay me."

Cecile walked back inside the cottage. The others were already at supper, talking excitedly about the ship and speculating as to what cargo might be left. She wished that she could share in the mood with the rest of them, but she couldn't help feeling that someone in the family should be practical.

"I will go back into the city tomorrow," her father was saying, "to see what can be saved from the ship. I'll need Benjamin, so you won't be able to finish the plowing just yet. Just work on what's already started."

"Oh, Father, why work at all?" cried Josette. "Soon we'll be rich again and we won't ever have to work again for the rest of our lives!"

"Now don't plan too much," Fabre admonished, "we don't know what will come from this ship." But the look in his eyes said that he, too, was making plans for the money they hadn't yet received.

"Will you at least bring us presents from the city?" Josette asked.

"Of course. What would you want?"

Her response was immediate. "An emerald necklace!"

Marie followed quickly with, "A pearl bracelet!"

"And what do you want, Cecile?"

She was going to answer that she wanted nothing, realizing that even if there was money to be made from the ship, he could never afford more than those two gifts. When she hesitated to reply, her father began to look both irritated and anxious, and nodded to her, waiting for her answer.

"A rose," she said finally.

"Oh how stupid," Marie muttered.

"Well, she never did have any class," said Josette.

Fabre seemed confused. "All you want is a rose?"

"Roses don't grow out here, and I would like to see one again."

Marie said, "Well, if she's going to ask for such a silly gift, then give it to her and use the money for our presents."

"Yes, Father," Cecile agreed. "Save any money you can. When you come back enormously rich, I'll ask for something else."

After dinner, as Cecile was clearing the table because her sisters were too exhausted from the good news to help, Gerard came back to talk to her.

"Now, little sister, tell me why you aren't as excited as the rest of us about Father's ship."

She wrung out the dishcloth and wiped up the crumbs from the table. "If Father comes back from the city with his saddle bags full of presents and money, then I'll be excited."

"But not before then?"

"No, not before."

Gerard laughed a bit too soberly to be jovial and kissed her lightly on the forehead. "Sometimes I think you're a little too practical to be a girl."

She slapped him playfully with the dishcloth. "If you're not going to help, then get out of my kitchen."

He stopped in the doorway. "Don't you even at least wish we might be rich again?"

She smiled and nodded. "I wish for a lot of things."

It was very late when she went to bed that night, yet she was the first one awake the next morning. There was too much worry on her mind to allow her to sleep well, so she got out of bed to begin breakfast and set about packing things for her father. He came out of his room as soon as he heard her shuffling about in the kitchen.

"Cecile, why are you up so early?"

"Well, I couldn't sleep because I kept thinking about what might happen today, so I thought I'd get started a little early. I've packed a lunch for you, and breakfast is just about done."

Fabre yawned and nodded. "Thank you, dear. I'll go and wake the rest of the family."

By the time Josette and Marie managed to powder and primp themselves enough to be seen, breakfast was set at the table and everyone else was seated. The talk consisted only of their father's impending journey and what riches would come of it. Only Cecile sat still, quietly eating her breakfast as the others made grand plans that she feared would ultimately come to nothing. A nagging sense of dread refused to leave her, and set her apart from the happiness the rest of her family was feeling.

Edmond and Victor left the table early to harness Benjamin, and Josette and Marie, after repeating their request for presents from the city, went back to bed. Gerard and Cecile were left alone with their father.

Gerard turned to him and said with a smile, "Well now, Father, I hope everything is well in the city. Good luck."

"I'm sure everything will be fine." He looked up at Cecile, who was quietly clearing the table, and asked, "Don't you wish me luck as well?"

"Of course I do, Father. I hope all turns out well."

"And are you sure all you want is a rose?"

"Yes, I'm certain. All I need is for you to come back to us safely, and soon. Then, if we have the money that all of you think we will, perhaps I will want an emerald necklace or a pearl bracelet. But for now, your return and the rose will be a perfectly acceptable gift." She gave him a quick hug. "Go and get dressed for the road. I believe everyone is anxious for you to be on your way."

Chapter Two

"Gerard, if they don't get out of that bed within ten minutes, I'm going to set fire to it!" Cecile warned, her patience at an end.

He laughed. "Well, that might get their attention."

"I'm not joking!" Cecile almost shouted, so frustrated she could barely breathe. "And you're not much better. I can't be the only one in this house who is working. I need some help! Father has only been gone a few weeks, and just look at the state of this place!"

The little farm truly was becoming unkempt. Cecile had kept up with the housework as best she could, but that meant the garden had suffered. Her sisters had never done any work, so that frustration was nothing new; but this sudden unconcerned attitude in her brothers was wearing on her. With each new weed that sprang up in that garden, her patience was stretched that much thinner.

"When was the last time you even set foot in the garden? Or Victor? Or Edmond?" she was raising her voice again, but couldn't help it.

"Cecile," said Gerard, a note of warning in his voice. He hated it when she scolded him, and indeed, it was a little ridiculous with her being so much younger. To their credit, it was a rare occasion for Cecile to be cross with him and rare when he deserved it. She worshipped him and he knew it, her tall, handsome brother. He was her refuge, and protected her from a lot of the harsh sniping of her sisters. And now, to keep this from becoming a fight, he took a deep breath and said calmly, "Please just relax a little, all right? Yes, Father has been gone several weeks…which means he'll be back shortly. Now I don't see the need to put all that much work into this place when we'll be leaving it soon. So just calm down a little."

He said everything so blithely that Cecile didn't quite know what to do with him. "But Gerard…"

"Relax," he cut her off. Then, tousling her hair with infuriating joviality, said, "I mean it. It's just no use ordering us to do the work that's quickly becoming unimportant."

She gazed up at his strong, handsome face with its lazy smile and wanted to throttle him. But instead, she shook her head in resignation. "All right. All right." Then, with a wicked grin that worried her eldest brother, she said, "I'll relax. Thank you, Gerard." With that, she turned and walked back into the house.

She went straight to her room and sat down on the bed. Then, with a self-satisfied sigh, she opened her book and settled into her pillows.

For most of the day she was there, reading and napping, and generally being lazier than she had been in over a year. Towards evening, she emerged long enough to put together a quick plate of dinner for herself, and then returned to her room. Her siblings milled about the table for a while, until they realized she wasn't going to feed them. Confused and hungry, they searched the kitchen but found little as Cecile was in the habit of making things fresh daily.

The next morning, Victor appeared at her bedroom door looking pathetic. "How about a little breakfast, Ceci?"

"No thanks. I already had some," she replied, barely looking up from her book.

Victor sighed and walked away. A little later, Cecile heard quite a bit of movement in the cottage and noticed through her window that Gerard and Edmond were in the garden. She watched them for a little while. They both looked miserable, but she wasn't ready to feel sorry for them just yet. Instead, she sat in her chair and began brushing her hair.

In the early hours of the afternoon, Gerard pounded on her door and then let himself into the room without waiting for her invitation. "Are you going to fix dinner tonight?"

She stretched languidly. "Oh, I don't know. I thought I'd relax a little."

"I *get* it, Cecile," he told her. "And I'm sure you noticed that we worked today. You can inspect the garden: there's not a weed to be found. The animals have been fed, cows milked, there's wood cut and ready for the fireplace...Marie-Elise was even seen with a dusting cloth in her hand."

"Did she do anything with it?"

"She did indeed, although I won't vouch for how good a job she did." He sighed and placed his hand over his heart in a melodramatic gesture, "Now have we earned your forgiveness? Will you please feed your poor starving family?"

With a laugh, she jumped up and hugged him, glad the fight was over. "Yes, and I'll even cook something you'll like!"

"That's my girl!"

"Oh Gerard, I've been so bored! I don't know how Josette and Marie do this every day."

He shoved her out of the room, laughing. "Well, I'm glad you've suffered too."

The look of relief on the faces of her brothers was almost comical. Edmond immediately handed her a basket of vegetables, and Victor was standing in the kitchen next to a pail of milk and the bags of meal, salt, and sugar he had carefully arranged on the table.

"You are the only one who knows what to do with these things!" Victor cried pitifully.

The girls were in the sitting room, pointedly ignoring what was happening in the kitchen, although they were as hungry as anyone was. Cecile glanced at them and rolled her eyes, but gave her brothers a smile.

"All right, then. Gerard, start the fire; Victor, bring in some water; and Edmond…there is a wheel of cheese in the larder, under the blue cloth."

They followed her orders without a moment's hesitation. She looked to her sisters and said in a steady voice, "If you'd like me to make enough for you as well, you'll set the table tonight."

She didn't wait to see their reactions, but started chopping vegetables immediately, perhaps feeling a bit stronger with the knife in her hands. It was no secret that her sisters, Josette in especial, despised her. But to her surprise, she heard tin plates and cups being slammed down onto the table. Cecile didn't turn around, not wanting them to see her triumphant smile.

In very short order, she had put together a nice vegetable soup and stacked a tower of cornmeal cakes. She skimmed the milk and poured it into a pitcher, resolving to make something sweet with the cream as a peace offering. Her brothers waited eagerly for the food to be set on the table, asking just a little too often if she needed their help with anything. Finally, she was forced to ask them just to sit and wait patiently.

The mood was jovial, saving her sisters. Everyone left them their own space at the table, preferring to gather close together to talk and laugh rather than share in the girls' stony silence.

"Well, Ceci," Edmond said through a mouthful of cornbread, "I'm so glad that tiff is over. I thought *I* was going to have to learn how to cook!"

They laughed, and Cecile told him, "It probably wouldn't hurt you to learn a little 'kitchen-craft'. Otherwise, I can hold you all hostage whenever I wish!"

"But you wouldn't do that," Gerard said, putting his arm around her. "You couldn't stand to see us suffer for that long."

"Oh, probably not. I would just have to forgive you all over again."

They were laughing and making jokes about how they each thought their own cooking would taste, when suddenly the door opened and in stepped their father.

After a stunned moment, Cecile jumped to her feet. "Father!" she cried. "Oh, it's so wonderful to have you back!" She ran and hugged him, followed closely by her brothers.

But he didn't look happy, and the smile he gave them seemed weary and forced. He placed his pack beside the chair and took off his cloak, then sat down heavily. Cecile brought him some water and sat next to him. "Is everything all right, Father?"

Josette looked out of the window, and then turned to her father impatiently. "Where is the coach? My things are packed and I'm ready to leave this awful place!"

"Well, you can unpack," Fabre said with a sigh. "There isn't any money left."

The room was deathly silent until Marie whined, "Didn't you even get us our presents?"

"I got Cecile's present," he said, reaching into his breast pocket and removing the rose. He held it out to her, his fingers shaking. "Little you know what it cost me."

She reached out and took it from him. Every aspect of it was perfection. Each burgundy petal curled out gently from the center, emitting a wondrous fragrance. She drifted her fingers over its velvety softness and said, "Thank you, Father. It's lovely."

Gerard took the seat next to his father and asked, "How is it that there is no more money? Was there a mistake? Did the ship not survive?"

"Oh the ship survived," said Fabre, "but the cargo wasn't so lucky. Much of it was damaged quite heavily. I sold what I could, and managed to pay off all of our creditors. I hope it is some consolation to you that we are no longer in debt."

"That's wonderful, Father," said Cecile. Indeed, it was more than she had hoped for.

But the others had set their hopes quite high. Marie burst into tears and threw herself into Josette's arms, and Josette simply looked at her father coldly. Edmond, at a loss for anything else to do, filled a plate and handed it to Fabre.

"Thank you, son. But now I have to tell you what happened on my way back home, and why I have to leave you again."

They circled around him, looking anxious. He took a deep breath and began, "I started home late in the afternoon, not wanting to spend any more money on lodging than I already had. I thought I'd be able to ride through the night, but it began to rain. Soon, the storm was in full gale, and I moved to the trees to try to block some of the wind, but lost my way in the darkness. Still, I continued on until a crash of thunder frightened the horse and he bolted. When I finally regained control, we were at the gate of a huge castle. I thought it must be abandoned, since there are no nobles out here, and decided I could take shelter there until the storm subsided.

"But it wasn't abandoned. The door opened for me, yet there was no one on the other side. I called out for someone, but no one answered. A light appeared from a room down the corridor, so I went in, but no one was there either. The fireplace was roaring, and a table was set for dinner, laden with food. On it was a note that welcomed me and bid me dine and stay the night. I didn't understand what was happening, but I was so tired and hungry that I stayed. As soon as I finished dinner, I heard another door opening, and entered it to find a bedchamber. It was quite warm and beautiful, and I slept very well.

"The next morning I awoke to a full breakfast, and went out to find Benjamin saddled and ready to go. I thanked the unseen host, although still nobody had appeared, and started out. But as I passed by the trellis I noticed the lovely roses, and thought that at least I might get one of the presents I promised."

He shuddered and looked at Cecile. "As soon as I had picked it, I heard a terrible roar. This…this…*creature*…appeared, rushing at me. It was terrifying. He was enormous, monstrous, hideous. It took the rose from my hand and shouted, 'How dare you steal from me after all I have done for you!'

"I tried to apologize, but the monster wouldn't let me speak. He said I was a thief. He said he was going to kill me. I told him…I told him everything that had happened to us. I told him that you had asked for this rose, and nothing else. And he said…he said…" he trailed off and gulped at his water.

"Yes, Father?" Cecile pushed, "what did he say?"

"He said that if you were to take my place, he wouldn't kill me."

"*What?!*" gasped Cecile.

He nodded. "Yes. He said that if I brought you to him, he would let me live. And then he let me go. But I have to return to him tomorrow. So I am only here to say good-bye." He was staring at his daughter intently, his gaze burning into her troubled eyes.

"Why did you have to ask for such an idiotic present!?" Josette screamed at Cecile, breaking the silence of the room. "This is all your fault!" She ripped the rose out of Cecile's hands and hit her with it, digging scratches into her sister's cheek.

"Shut up, Josette!" Gerard yelled, pushing her away and drawing Cecile to him. "No one will go to this monster because we will kill it."

Their father finally stood. "No, you can't kill it. He's too powerful. I refuse to lose any of my children to him."

Marie looked shocked. "You mean you're not going to send Cecile?"

"Of course he's not going to send Cecile!" Gerard shouted, holding his youngest sister even more tightly. Victor and Edmond flanked him, each putting a protective hand on Cecile.

"But she's the one who started all of this!"

"It was her stupid rose!"

Gerard was horrified. "I can't believe you! Cecile is *not* going!"

"Yes, I am," she said quietly.

Her brothers backed away suddenly, surprise on their faces.

"You can't mean that," Gerard said earnestly.

"I do mean it."

Her father reached for her hand. "You don't have to do this, Cecile."

She squeezed the hand in hers. "I can be responsible for my own life, but I can't be responsible for yours."

He looked both pained and…relieved. With a heavy sigh, he turned away from them and went into his room, closing the door behind him.

Josette's look was one of triumph, but Gerard was astounded. He looked at his brothers and said, "How could he just walk away like that?"

Cecile, too, walked quietly into her room. She shut the door and fell against it, trembling. What began as mere tremors soon escalated until she was unable to breathe. Her father's story, the castle, the monster…it couldn't be happening. He must have been ill, or drunk, or dreaming.

Two great tears spilled down her cheeks and she took several deep, shuddering breaths in order to keep the tears from turning into weeping.

"Calm down, Cecile," she said aloud. "You'll go tomorrow and maybe…maybe you won't find anything. Nothing at all. Then you'll come back home and everything will be all right."

She swiped her hands across her face and took a deep breath before returning to the kitchen. But there was a cold, cutting voice within her that told her she would find the castle, her father was totally sane and sober, and that a horrible beast would be waiting to kill her.

Chapter Three

At dawn the next morning, Gerard went to Cecile's room. She was awake, still lying in bed. Burgundy rose petals were spread haphazardly over her quilt.

He sat down on the edge of her bed. "Cecile, please don't do this. Please don't go to that castle," he begged her quietly.

"Would you rather Father went?"

"No, I'd rather we killed this creature."

"That's unreasonable," she admonished softly.

"So is your decision."

"Please don't make me feel guilty about this, Gerard. This whole situation is my fault."

He shook his head. "Don't let Marie and Josette make you feel that way," he whispered back to her. "It isn't your fault."

"Why did I ask for that stupid rose?" she asked, her eyes filling with tears. "Why did I do that? I could have asked for a necklace. But I didn't want him to feel bad when there wasn't enough money. And now look what I've done."

"It's not your fault, Cecile. Please don't go."

She wiped her eyes roughly, fighting the urge to weep uncontrollably. Then she picked up several sheets of paper and said, "I've written down the instructions for the things I do around here. Recipes and things like that. I hope it'll help. And here," she said, handing him her treasured book, "this is for you...to remember me by."

Gerard took the book and hugged her tightly. "I couldn't forget you, silly girl."

Then Victor and Edmond were at her door. "Ceci, are you really going to go away?"

"Yes, I'm going. So hug me, quick!"

They all sat on her bed, holding her tightly until she made them leave so she could get ready to go. Her father was at the table, dressed for traveling, when she finally emerged from her room.

"Father, I told you that I would go."

"I'm going with you. If you change your mind, then I will stay and you will come back here."

She shook her head slowly, but didn't argue with him. Her brothers hugged her so tightly she didn't think they'd ever let her go, but Marie and Josette pecked at her cheek and returned to their room, where she was certain she heard them laugh. Gerard looked at their door and glowered, but gave Cecile another kiss.

"Good-bye, Ceci."

But she couldn't say good-bye. She climbed up onto the horse and closed her eyes as Benjamin began walking.

It was evening by the time they arrived at the gates of the castle, and she and her father had barely spoken. The trees had opened before them, guiding their path through the forest straight up to the immense castle doors.

"You can go back home now, Cecile," her father offered quietly.

"No. I'm staying."

He sighed and helped her off of Benjamin's broad back. Cecile hugged the horse's neck and kissed his soft muzzle. "I'm going to miss you," she whispered, giving him a final pat.

Fabre led her to the castle and pushed the heavy door open and walked in. Sconces lit the way to the dining room, where a small round table was set with dinner for two. He took off his cloak and threw it across a chair. "The food in this place is quite wonderful," he said, forcing a smile.

She looked with wonder at everything around her. The small room was marvelous. Paintings and faded tapestries lined the walls and every piece of furniture was ornately carved. 'So,' she thought, 'this is where I shall die. It is a pretty place.'

She sat down opposite her father and ate her dinner, finding herself to be surprisingly hungry. Everything was, indeed, quite wonderful. She had never thought to eat food so rich again. Although she tried to sound pleasant, her father hardly said a word. Then the harsh echo of heavy footsteps clanged throughout the corridors of the castle, freezing her heart.

The door opened, casting a large, dark shadow across the table. The shadow eclipsed as the door was closed again. "Good evening," said a deep, gruff, terrible voice.

Cecile turned around and gasped. He was far worse than any adjective her father had used could have prepared her for. He was very tall, with massive shoulders. Out of his shaggy brown hair grew two large curving ram-like horns. Shorter hair seemed to cover the rest of his body, although Cecile couldn't be certain of that because he was dressed in the clothing and jewelry of a nobleman. His huge hands had long claws jutting out of the unusually long fingers and the large teeth that his black lips could not quite conceal looked even more deadly than the claws.

When his gaze rested on Cecile, he seemed, for a moment, to be faint. With a gruff but hushed voice he said, "Truly you are beautiful." Then sternness took over and he asked stiffly, "Have you come willingly?"

"Yes, I have. The rose my father took was for me." Her voice was almost inaudible.

"And you will stay here with me?"

"Yes."

"And you will promise never to ask me if you may go home. This is your home now. Do you promise?"

"Yes."

"Swear it."

"I swear. I promise I'll never ask to go home."

The creature closed his eyes and breathed heavily. "Then you are a thousand times more beautiful than I first thought you. From now on you shall be called Beauty."

"And what should I call you?" she asked.

His expression grew harsh. "I am the Beast."

Cecile trembled but the Beast simply turned to her father. "I am pleased with her. She can stay. And you, loving father," he said mockingly, "who so willingly trades in his own child, you will leave tomorrow at dawn. You will take with you two trunks filled with precious things so that you will have gifts as precious as your *memory* of Beauty, for she is mine now." He walked to the door, but gave her one last look before he left. "Good night, Beauty."

As the door closed, she released a shuddering breath. "Oh, Father!"

He held onto her hand tightly. She was losing her resolve quickly, and she closed her eyes and took several deep, calming breaths. They stayed up all night, talking about anything that came to mind. Cecile talked constantly, nearly losing her voice by dawn, because she knew that if she stopped to think about what she was doing, she wouldn't go through with it. She knew in her heart that these would be the last hours she'd spend with her father...that the Beast might kill her. She tried not to think about that, so she talked about light and unimportant things--nonsense, but it made her feel better. The sunrise, however, brought her back to reality. It was the most depressing dawn she had ever in her life witnessed.

They knew when it was time for him to leave. Two huge, ornate trunks appeared in the room. "Look, Father!"

He opened up one of the trunks. It was filled to the top with gold and silver coins, diamonds, and on top of all of this sat an emerald necklace and a pearl bracelet.

"He has made you rich again," Cecile said, picking up a few of the coins.

Her father shook his head. "He's mocking me. There's no way to carry these." He knocked the lid down and took Cecile's hand. They walked down the corridor together, the doors opening as they neared them. Outside was Benjamin, and beside him stood a small pack-horse, both trunks strapped to his back as if they weighed nothing.

"Oh my goodness," Cecile breathed.

Her father turned to her, his eyes lighting up. "Perhaps this Beast is not as bad as he seems. He is very generous."

Cecile looked very hurt, so he added, "But I would rather be poor and have you, than be rich without you."

A rumble echoed through the castle, and they knew his departure couldn't be put off any longer. She helped him with his cloak, and then gave him a quick hug. Smiling as naturally as possible, for she didn't want her father's last memory of her to be of tears, she said, "Good-bye, Father. Give my love to everyone."

"Good-bye, Cecile."

She watched him leave, then stood for a very long time just staring at the gates. Then the tears came. She could no longer hold them back. She sat down on the steps, placed her head in her hands, and wept more bitterly than she ever had before. She cried until she made herself sick, then she walked back inside and curled up in one of the large chairs in the dining room and cried herself to sleep. She didn't know that the Beast had been watching her.

She awoke around noon with her back aching from sleeping in such a cramped position. The table had been set with a light lunch, but she couldn't bring herself to eat any of it. She walked out of the dining room and to the first open door. Above the doorway was scripted in silver '*Beauty's Room*'. Her bedroom.

Inside was a beautiful four-poster curtained feather bed covered with quilts and soft comforters. A dressing table stood in one corner and a large armchair was set before the fireplace. Sunlight filtered through the French doors which opened to a very small balcony.

Cecile looked around in wonder. She went from one object to another, examining everything. A magnificent jeweled dress lay draped across the bed. She looked at it and shuddered. Although everything was splendid, it frightened her. What kind of prisoner was she to be, with such beautiful surroundings?

She stayed in her room until dinner, afraid of meeting up with the Beast should she step outside her door. However, she was ravenous by the time evening arrived, so she carefully looked in both directions down the corridor, then, seeing no one, walked quickly to the dining room. Again, the table was set only for her, but this time it was a very large supper which included some of her favorite foods.

It wasn't until she was just finishing her dinner that the door opened and a terrible shadow filled the room. Cecile dropped her spoon and closed her eyes.

"Good evening, Beauty. May I sit down?"

She nodded, but trembled with fear and disgust as he sat down across from her at the small round table. After a moment, he asked roughly, "Didn't you see your new gown?"

"Yes."

"I wish you would wear it."

"I don't want it."

He sighed heavily, and Cecile expected an argument, but he didn't say anything more about it. Several minutes passed before he spoke again. "Are you happy here?"

"How could I be happy here?" she asked, wishing her voice sounded stronger. The fact that he was being so calm and quiet frightened her more than if he had growled and blustered.

"I tried to make my castle as interesting as possible. But then, you didn't see much of my castle today, did you?"

Cecile raised her eyes to stare at him, but knew she couldn't hold that stare for long. "Are you going to hurt me?" she asked.

The Beast shook his head slowly, his horns glistening in the glow of the fire. "No. I will never, ever hurt you," he said earnestly.

"You're not going to kill me?"

"No. You are in no danger from me. I'll never hurt you."

She wanted to ask him more questions: why then was she here? How long did he intend to keep her? There were so many. But she couldn't bring herself to ask them. More than anything, she wished he'd go away. Yet he stayed, staring at her. She could feel his eyes on her although she had long since dropped her gaze.

"Beauty," he said finally, "you think I'm very ugly, don't you?" He cocked his head to one side.

What a strange question for him to ask. She shuddered and looked away from him. "Yes, I do. But I try never to judge by appearances."

He made a sudden movement and she cringed, half expecting him to strike her. But he didn't. He laughed. "Oh really? And yet my ugliness frightens you and you think I'm terrible."

Cecile felt anger and indignation burning though her. "You frighten me because you threatened my father and demanded my life!"

The Beast sank down into his chair, surprise and shame evident on his face. "I'm sorry. Yes, I am very ugly, and terrible. But I have a good heart. You have nothing to fear from me." He could see that her eyes were filling up with tears. "Please don't cry, my Beauty. Only trust that I need you here, and I will do everything I can for you."

Looking into his dark eyes, the only beautiful thing about his appearance, she knew that she could trust him. He wouldn't lie to her…he had no need to.

"Yes. I trust you."

His breathing eased. "Good. That means very much to me. Now, would you mind if I come to visit you in the evenings, after you have finished dining?"

"If that is what you wish."

"Beauty, it isn't what *I* wish, but what *you* wish that matters here. You are the mistress of this castle, and I will give you everything within my power."

Cecile looked away. His gaze made her uncomfortable. Then he asked a question that could not have possibly been even in her darkest nightmares.

"Beauty, will you marry me?"

She sucked in her breath so hard that it hurt.

"Just answer yes or no," the Beast ordered terribly.

"No." Her voice wavered, but she looked up defiantly.

The Beast closed his eyes, and a low, rumbling growl began in his chest but emerged as a whimper. He stood up abruptly and walked toward her. Then his huge and terrible clawed hand reached out to her, and dropped a rose onto her empty plate. "Good night, Beauty. Sleep well." And he walked to the door, casting one long glance toward her before he stepped through the doorway and was gone.

Chapter Four

She sat at the edge of the balcony, peering through the railing at the grounds stretching out below. The fragrance of roses mingled with a number of other flowers and drifted over the balcony, caressing her skin. The moon was very low and very bright, illuminating statues and fountains, courtyards and gardens. Nothing, however, was beautiful in her eyes. The cold stone and iron of a prison cell would have evoked the same feelings in her. Cecile felt a chill descend upon her as the Beast parted the lace curtains which hung in front of the glass doors and stepped outside to join her.

"Beauty, nothing on the table has been touched, not even the water. And you didn't eat anything at breakfast...or at noon." He sounded concerned.

"I'm not hungry."

"Are you ill?"

"No."

"Do you dislike what is served?"

She sighed heavily and closed her eyes, hugging the post she was leaning against. She should tell him to stop coming every night. "Please just leave me alone."

He was silent for several long moments, but she knew he was still there. Finally, he said, "Beauty, you have been here for three days. Why won't you wear the gown I've given you?"

Cecile stood and smoothed out her rumpled skirt. In defiance, she had worn her old dress every day, ignoring the fabulous gown she had found in her room. It still lay draped over the chair on which she had placed it that very first day.

"If I eat something, will you go away?" she asked coldly.

The Beast leaned against the wall and bowed his head. "Yes," he said softly, as if the word was very heavy, "I will leave if you'll eat something."

Holding her breath, she walked quickly past him into the dining room and took a piece of bread from the table. After holding it up for him to see, she turned away so she wouldn't have to look at him while she ate it. The bread was soft and white, and very fresh, but tonight it stuck in her throat as if she were trying to swallow mud. Too much weeping. Her throat was sore, stomach ached, head pounded. She had never been so miserable.

"There are many things here in my castle for you," he said as he walked in after her. "I wish you would find them. I think you would like it here if only you'd find them." He paused again, waiting for a reply from her. There wasn't one. "You aren't confined to your room. Why do you remain there all day?"

"You said you would go away," she insisted.

"Yes, and I will go."

He walked up to her and held out a rose. Cecile stared at it, unmoved, feeling all of her muscles clench. Sheer perfection had kissed each peach-colored petal, but she wouldn't take it. Not from his fingers. After only a few moments, he released the stem and the flower fell to the floor.

"Will you marry me?"

"No." She spat out the word, but refused to look at him. Her stare was locked onto the emerald brooch pinned into the lace at his throat.

He did not turn to go. "But Beauty, there is truly no need for you to stay confined to your room. My castle is open to you. In it, you may do anything you wish."

It was too much. Something inside of her snapped and she lunged for the knife at the table. Gripping its handle so tightly that her knuckles turned white, she rounded on him, the silver blade glistening in the candlelight. "And if I wished to kill you?" she demanded.

Very slowly, very deliberately—his eyes never leaving her face—he sank his claws through the delicate white silk of his shirt and pulled it open to expose his shaggy chest. "Strike true," his voice rumbled, "at my heart."

A very small, wild, panicked part of her was ready to do it. Sink the knife straight through that broad chest, and then run. Run away. Run home. With a cry, she threw the knife across the room where it clattered uselessly against the stone floor. "I hate you."

His voice was soft. "You don't know me."

"I hate this place."

"You know nothing about it."

Cecile turned her face to the wall. "Please go away. Please. Please just go away."

"I'm sorry. I—"

"*Go away!*"

She heard him sigh, then listened to the sound of his footsteps taking him away from her.

For the next several days, Cecile remained in her bedroom almost constantly; running to the dining room quickly when she was hungry, but never staying long enough for the Beast to see her. Otherwise, she stayed in bed, feeling miserable and petulant and hating herself for it. And hating the Beast, too.

Then one morning, as she sat staring out of her bedroom window, she heard a strange but enchanting melody, as if an angel's music box had been opened just outside her door. It seemed to be calling to her, and although she tried, she couldn't resist it. She got up and opened her door, but the melody retreated down the corridor.

"Well, go on, Pandora," she muttered to herself, "open your box."

The castle seemed dark and gloomy and depressing to her as she looked down the shadowy hallway. She turned and followed the music to a large set of oak doors. On each door was carved a single rose. The carvings were undeniably beautiful: very intricate and detailed. She placed her hand against a door and pushed. Inside was a large gallery of paintings. Every upper class family in the city had a gallery of some sort, but this was the most immense one Cecile had ever seen in her life. There were pictures of all sorts of subjects on every wall, but very few portraits, which seemed odd to her. She didn't spend much time contemplating it, however, for the landscapes had captured her attention. No longer needing a melody to coax her through, she wandered deep into the gallery.

One painting--a little farm scene--caught her notice, and soon she found she couldn't look away from it. It was consuming her concentration as she tried to focus on the subjects, but realized she couldn't. It was impossible to keep her eyes on them, almost as if they were moving. She leaned in closer. They *were* moving. She felt as if she were looking through a window rather than gazing at a painting. There were men working in the fields, wagons being driven over the roads, children and animals playing. It was impossible. Cecile reached out and touched her finger to it, but felt only paint and canvas; and yet the movement continued. She could even see the wheat field moving with the breeze.

"Oh my goodness," she breathed. "How is this possible?"

Intrigued, she ran through the gallery, looking for other such paintings. She found several, including a masquerade that held her attention for quite some time. It was beautiful, full of bright costumes and fanciful masks. The dancers were graceful and artistic, and Cecile could even see the flicker of the candles in the chandelier.

She stopped short at the largest of the paintings in the gallery. It stood half the height of the wall, was brilliantly painted, and was a portrait of her. She examined it carefully, barely breathing. This was no coincidental look-alike...this was *her*. Every detail was perfect, from the flecks of cool grey in her green eyes, to the copper-colored curls. Even the few freckles she had acquired from working in the sun this past year were placed perfectly. Without looking at anything else, Cecile turned and left the gallery, her heart pounding.

The music was waiting for her at another set of doors. She had barely laid her fingers against the heavy oak when they swung open, as if they had been waiting impatiently for her to enter. The room revealed by their parting was enormous, and filled floor to ceiling with a maze of shelves. Each shelf was stacked with hundreds of books and manuscripts. A library. Cecile walked through the room, running her hands along the shelves as if in a dream. She had never seen so many books in one place before, and it thrilled her. She turned in circles, looking up at the towering shelves. There were more books here than she could read in a lifetime...thousands of manuscripts at her fingertips. Some of her old favorites were there, and she went so far as to sit right down on the floor below the bookshelves and enjoy a few pages from them.

"Perhaps this isn't quite as much a prison as I'd thought," she said to herself, closing and re-shelving a book of poetry.

She tried several other doors--all of them locked--before she came to one that opened for her. Inside was a very small room, filled with tapestry racks, threads of all colors, and needles of many different sizes. Cecile smiled as she walked inside. It had been a very long time since she'd been able to sew just for the pleasure of it. One small needlepoint had already been started; across the top, the words "Beauty's Sewing Room" had been embroidered.

The last room she explored contained the most beautiful piano she had ever seen. She gave a squeal of delight and rushed to it. She hadn't played since she'd had to sell her own beloved piano over a year ago, and she had missed it dreadfully. Sheets of music rested on the instrument, which bore the words "Beauty's Piano".

Without a thought for her midday meal, Cecile sat down and played the music provided until night fell and she was obliged to light the candles so that she could find her way back down the corridor. She hadn't realized how hungry she was until she passed the dining room. Then the aroma of delicious food flooded out and drew her inside, but she stopped before she sat down. Her dress really was looking old and rumpled. With a deep breath, she turned and walked back to her room.

After carefully folding her peasant's dress, she took the jeweled gown from the chair and held it out in front of her. It truly was lovely, and richer than any she had ever owned. The silk fabric was the color of champagne, embroidered with diamonds and trimmed with an intricate lace. With a little imagination, she managed to dress herself and fasten all of the many hooks and laces.

When she turned to go out, she realized that a large wooden wardrobe had appeared in the room. Hesitantly, she opened its door and was greeted by a complete pallet of colors. There were gowns of different colors and fabrics; velvets, muslins, satins, Chinese silks…and all in deep blues and greens, purples, yellows, pastels. Some had vivid patterns; others were littered with jewels and laces. There were ostrich plumes and peacock feathers, ribbons and combs, all to be used in her hair. Shawls and capes, ranging from warm woolens to light laces, were hung on pegs. Satin and velvet slippers, sturdy leather shoes, and high-heeled boots lined the floor.

She laughed as she looked inside. "So, I've given in to one dress, and I inherit an entire wardrobe."

Cecile had just finished her dessert when the door to the dining room opened. But this time, the opening of the door was not so frightening, nor the shadow that fell from it so terrible.

"Good evening, Beauty."

It made her uncomfortable to be addressed as 'Beauty', but she said, "Good evening, Beast."

"Thank you for coming to dinner tonight, and for wearing the gown." He looked very pleased, and she knew the baring of his sharp teeth was a smile.

"You're welcome. Thank you for the wardrobe."

He nodded as he sat down in his chair. "How was your day?"

"I explored the castle today."

"I know. Do you still hate it?"

Just thinking about the things she had said and done the last time she had seen the Beast made her ashamed of herself. She swallowed hard and said, "No, I don't hate it. And I'm sorry about what I said before. It's beautiful here."

It was obvious that the apology had taken him by surprise, but he said, "It is much more beautiful now that you are here."

Cecile looked away, uneasy under his gaze.

"Are you feeling better?" he asked.

She nodded, feeling a little foolish about her many days spent in bed. "Yes. I am much better. I'll come to dinner from now on."

"Thank you." He stared at her for a little while before startling her with the question, "Beauty, why did you ask your father for a rose when your sisters asked for jewels?"

She reached for her goblet and drank deeply, her throat aching at the mention of her family. "Because he wanted me to ask for something, and I knew there wouldn't be money for jewels."

The Beast thought about her answer for a while. "Why was your face scratched when you first arrived here?"

"Because my sister Josette hit me. In fact, she hit me with that same rose."

She heard a growl in his chest, but he merely said, "Will you tell me about your life, Beauty?"

"My life?"

"Yes, your life. Your family. Everything." He sat back in the chair and folded his awful hands together, waiting. "I would like to learn some more about you."

She twisted her fingers into a lock of her hair, beginning to feel self-conscious. "Well...I have two sisters and three brothers. My mother died when I was very young. I don't remember very much about her. My father was a merchant, and with the money you gave him will probably be one again. I have been both rich and poor. I've lived in the city and the country. And...that is all."

"Did you get along with your family?"

"With my father, yes. And with my brothers. I miss them. My sisters were never very fond of me...although they were great friends with each other."

"And did that hurt?"

"Sometimes." Cecile fidgeted in her chair. This conversation was making her very uncomfortable. "Could we talk about something else?"

"Whatever you wish."

The first question that came to mind concerned those strange paintings. "Who put the paintings in the gallery?"

"I did."

"Who painted them?"

"Artists."

Neither the answer nor the tone of voice invited any more questions. Cecile stared at her plate.

"Did you enjoy your piano?"

"Very much. It's a pity I'm not a more talented musician."

"And do you enjoy sewing?"

She nodded. "Yes. I think I'll like that little room very much."

"Good. I'm glad I have found some things that might make you happy. I want very much for you to be happy here. Is there anything else you enjoy that I can get you?"

"But there is so much already."

"Anything." It was almost a demand.

"I like paints," she answered quickly.

"Very well."

Cecile put her napkin over her plate and glanced around the room, not sure of what to say to him. Finally, after another sip of wine, she said, "I really liked the library."

He smiled. "I thought you might, if only you would leave your room to enter it."

With a blush, she admitted, "Well, the music outside my door was a nice touch."

"It was all I could think of to entice you out of your room. I'm glad it worked."

They were silent again for a little while after that. Then the Beast leaned slightly forward and asked, "Beauty, will you marry me?"

Cecile shuddered. "What can I say?"

"Just answer yes or no. That's all."

"No."

The Beast breathed such a terrible sigh that she actually felt sorry for him. He heaved himself up and walked around the table to her. Then he dropped a rose onto her plate and said, "Good night, Beauty."

As the door closed, Cecile sighed her relief. The Beast did not seem as bad as he had at first, but she was still thankful that he evidently didn't plan to impose his company on her very often. She finished her drink and then got up from the table and walked to her bedroom.

It wasn't long before she found an easel with several canvasses, paint pots, and brushes stacked up around it.

Chapter Five

Over the next few weeks, Cecile explored the gardens and courtyards that surrounded the castle. At first, she remained outside to avoid encountering the Beast in the castle. But the wonders she found fascinated her so much that she became a true explorer. She hadn't realized just how massive the castle was until she walked its perimeter. It took her nearly an hour to walk all the way around the structure, and that made her even more curious as to what might be on the inside.

The courtyards were vast landscaped spaces with marble walkways and baroque fountains. All that she had found time to explore were incredibly beautiful, as if they were taken care of every day, but she never saw anyone else. The gardens were surrounded by stone walls and were full of flowers, statues, and marble benches. Most of them were built on a theme and in exploring them, Cecile felt as if she were walking through some of her favorite stories. One was an Oriental garden, with a little stream flowing between exotic flowers and trees, including a ginger tree that she immediately fell in love with. Another garden looked like it had sprung from the pages of the Arabian Nights. Its paths were made of blue and white mosaic tiles and on its grounds was an aviary shaped like a mosque. In yet another garden she found an Egyptian motif. Statues of Egyptian gods and goddesses were placed between pyramids and sphinxes, and a barge floated down a 'Nile'. Every sight seemed more magnificent than the last and Cecile found herself going outside every day to try to explore some new part of the Beast's grounds. At times she didn't understand the theme of a particular garden or courtyard, for it was based on a people or story she'd never heard of before. On these occasions, she would ask the Beast for an explanation, and therefore learned a new piece of literature or history.

She had found yet another new garden when she finally admitted to herself that this must be one of the most beautiful places in the world, and how good it was that she was able to enjoy it. It was amazing that such an ugly creature as the Beast could be responsible for such wonders.

As she walked along the path of this 'Greek' garden, she stopped to examine one of the statues. It stood with its white arms outstretched to her; impassive, unmoving. She walked up to it and brushed her cheek against its open palm, but it was smooth and silent and cold, and not the human touch she longed for. Until that moment, she had not realized how long it had been since she had felt the touch of someone else's hands. The Beast never touched her. For that she was thankful. She didn't know what the touch of the Beast might do to her.

Still, she climbed up onto the pedestal and put her arms around the statue, pretending that it was the warm, feeling touch she wanted. That made her depressed, and she rested her head against the stone neck and wept.

After only a few moments, she realized how silly she must look: hugging a statue and crying, and she had to laugh at herself. She kissed the stone cheek and said, "Thank you, sir, for being so understanding."

Climbing down, she vowed to be more sensible in the future. Instead of exploring the gardens further, she went back to the castle. The gardens always seemed to put her in an ethereal frame of mind, and she thought that might be her problem.

That evening, the Beast entered the room looking very concerned. He sat down and watched her in silence for a few moments, dispensing with his usual 'good evening'. "Beauty, are you very lonely here?"

She nodded slowly. "Yes."

"Why?"

At that question, she wanted to be angry with him, but when she looked into his eyes she realized that he wasn't being patronizing. Perhaps he didn't understand what this place was like for her. "I've never been alone before, and here, I'm alone all day long. There's no one to talk to. This castle, though beautiful, is a very lonely place."

"I'm sorry for that."

"Are we the only people here?" she asked. She knew that there must be someone else. Gardeners, chamber maids, cooks…things were so well cared for that she was certain there were others in this vast castle.

"Yes. There is only us."

She blinked, not sure that she believed him. "Then how is everything done?"

"It is simply done, my dear. Don't let it trouble you."

"But—"

"Beauty," he interrupted her, "do you remember when the wardrobe appeared in your room?"

Cecile hesitated. "Yes…"

"Did anyone enter your room and put it there?"

She shook her head.

"That is how things are done around here. Please, *don't let it trouble you.*"

"All right," she whispered.

He didn't stay very much longer, and seemed distracted throughout their meeting. And when Cecile walked past her sewing room on the way to bed, she heard a strange rattling inside. She pushed the door open and found a small white dove in a cage just inside the window. Intrigued, she walked in and read the inscription on the gilded cage:

Speak with me, I will hear
Every word you say, my dear
Tell me all the things you know
Past this room they will not go.

"Oh, Beast, that's so sweet," she breathed, a few tears escaping.

She had not yet begun her dessert the next evening when the door creaked open and Beast looked in. "I'm terribly sorry. You're still dining. Excuse me." He began backing out of the doorway.

"Beast, please come back in."

"But you are still dining."

"I'm almost finished. Sit down and talk to me."

He ventured inside a little further. "Won't you be sickened by having to look at me while you eat?"

"Of course not!" she said quickly, although she realized that if he had asked even just last night, her answer would have been different. The dove and everything it represented had made a change in her perception of him, and she said, "Don't talk that way about yourself."

"As you wish." He sat down across from her and folded his hands.

"I wanted to thank you…for the present."

He nodded. "It isn't what you wanted, but I'm afraid I can't deliver that. I'm sorry."

"No Beast…it's perfect." She smiled at him and realized with a pang of guilt that it was the first smile she had ever given him. "It's perfect."

He seemed pleased with himself.

She continued her supper, but felt increasingly uncomfortable at being the only one eating. Finally she asked, "May I serve you something to eat, Beast?"

He looked startled at the suggestion. "No...thank you."

"Are you sure? Perhaps something to drink?"

"No. That wouldn't be proper."

"But, Beast—"

He cut her off with a wave of his hand. Then he opened his mouth widely, exposing all of the horrible teeth. "I am not designed for civilized dining. I hunt when I wish to eat, and I do not use such things as knives and spoons. I will not subject you to the sight of me attempting this aspect of civilized society."

Cecile gripped her goblet tightly and asked very carefully, "What do you hunt?"

"There are animals on my land other than me."

"Do you enjoy this hunting?"

"*I hate it!*" The room echoed with his voice. He dropped his head into his hands, and then drew it back up again quickly, digging deep scratches into his face with his claws. "I frightened you. I'm sorry. I won't shout again."

She had been frightened, but as the blood seeped through his fur and slowly dripped down his face, that fear quickly turned to pity. Cecile wanted to help him, but the thought of touching him was repulsive to her. At a loss for anything else to do, she dipped her napkin into her water and handed it across the table to him. "You scratched yourself," she said in answer to his questioning look.

"Did I?" He took the very edge of the napkin and she quickly let go of it. Beast held it to his face and it came away stained with blood. "I'm sorry. That must look ghastly," he said with a light voice.

She smiled, glad that he was changing the tone of the conversation. "Oh, not ghastly, just painful."

After wiping his face with the damp cloth, Beast smiled back at her and flexed his fingers, showing the sharp claws. "I've scratched myself with these so often that I no longer even notice."

"You could cut them off," she suggested.

"They would only grow back," Beast said. He quickly changed the subject by telling her, "I found something for you to do tomorrow."

"Why?"

"Because I sense a storm coming on and you won't be able to go outside. You seem to spend so much time in the courtyards that I was afraid you were tiring of your other amusements. So if you're bored tomorrow, there is now a large jigsaw puzzle in the drawing room."

He thought of everything. "Oh Beast, you do so much for me."

"I would do anything for you."

"Would you let me see my family?" she asked quickly, hardly daring to look at him.

A look of pain entered his eyes, and she added, "I only want to see them for a moment. I miss them so much."

"You wish only to see them?" he asked cautiously.

"Yes. Only to see them. To see that they are all right."

He released a slow breath and said finally, "The mirror above your dressing table will show you whatever you wish to see."

"Thank you, Beast."

He left soon afterwards, sensing her eagerness to look into the mirror. Her family had moved back to the city, and as she watched them over the next few days, she was amazed to see how many changes had occurred in their lives without her. Josette had married a man she had once refused, but now that she was past the ideal marriageable age, she'd had to settle for him. Both Gerard and Marie were engaged. Gerard's fiancée was a young woman named Lavinia, whom Cecile remembered from the city, but she didn't know the man engaged to Marie. Her brothers were helping her father with his reborn shipping business, and all were very successful. It seemed that so much was happening while she was away, but she was grateful to Beast for giving her this window to her world.

And she found that the more time she spent in Beast's castle, the less she minded his appearance. It fact, as she spent so much time alone and he was so kind to her, she began to look forward to his visits. He did, in truth, do everything for her. When she became sick with a cold she found medicine of honey and lemon for her cough, and every meal included hot soup and oranges until she was feeling better. There was always chocolate for her, as if Beast somehow knew that it was her favorite. If something had upset her during the day, she would find a new piece of jewelry or bottle of perfume on her dressing table. And every evening when he came to see her, he had a rose for her.

Their conversations were always interesting, and Beast tried very hard to keep her entertained. Sometimes he made her laugh, for he could tell a story like no one she had ever known. Sometimes, however, he seemed so tragic that he brought her close to tears. It struck her as very odd, but once she stopped trying to hate him, she found that she actually did like him.

He must have noticed the change in her feelings, for one evening he asked openly, "Beauty, do you still feel uncomfortable when I am with you?"

She considered many different replies, but as always when speaking with Beast, the truth seemed to be the best option. She knew that he would see through any film of flattery she might use. "Sometimes…but just a little. Actually, those times are growing less and less frequent."

"Do you know why that is so?"

She looked thoughtful for a few moments. "Because I feel more and more that you are my friend."

Beast smiled at her. "What can I do to make you feel more comfortable?"

"It makes me uncomfortable when you call me Beauty," she answered firmly.

He cocked his head to one side and stared at her thoughtfully. "Do you not consider yourself to be beautiful?"

"No, not really. The thought never occurred to me."

"Why not?"

How to answer such a straightforward question? She shrugged and said, "I don't know. My sisters always told me how plain I was… 'God-awful plain' is how Josette used to put it. And next to them, I do look plain. It was always just an accepted fact that I wasn't good enough to go out with them. I suppose I've always taken that as a pretty firm indication that I wasn't beautiful."

Beast considered that for a moment, then commented, "I do not think I would like your sisters very much. But know that you *are* beautiful—more than others because you do not need powders and frills to make you so."

"Thank you," she said quietly.

"And it is good that after so long, there is a thing of beauty here to balance my horrid ugliness."

Cecile bit her lip.

"Did your father never do anything to stop your sisters from speaking to you so unkindly?"

"My brothers were always quick to come to my defense. Especially Gerard. He was my champion."

"But not your father?"

"No."

"Why not?"

She didn't look up. "Because my father is…" she had never before added the word to her troubled thoughts, "…weak."

Beast raised his shaggy eyebrows, but said nothing.

"If he wasn't weak, he wouldn't have allowed my sisters to bully me. He would have been stronger against our creditors. He would have fought the bankruptcy. He would have made everyone pull their own weight at the cottage. And he would never have permitted me…" she trailed off. The words felt like a betrayal, but she knew that they were true.

It was Beast who finished the thought for her. "To take his place."

Cecile tasted acid in her throat. "Yes."

"I'm sorry," said Beast.

"*It was my rose*," Cecile insisted. "And even if he had said no, I would have come anyway."

Beast nodded and leaned forward. "Because you're a good, brave girl."

"I just wish he would have said no." She blinked away her tears.

"Of course you do. But you love him anyway, because it is your nature. That is beautiful. And you are truly deserving of the name 'Beauty'. When I first gave you this name, it was for two reasons: your appearance, of course, and your willingness to remain with one such as me. But since then, I've found so many more reasons to believe that the name suits you that I couldn't begin to think of calling you anything else. So please, grant me the favor of calling you by the name I find most fitting."

"All right," she conceded, "but can't I call you anything other than Beast?"

He shook his head. "Beast is the only name I deserve."

It frightened her whenever he spoke that way about himself. He had always been kind and gentle, and very patient in her presence. There was no question that he looked beastly, but she was certain that he had a soul. "Why do you say that? You don't seem to be a beast to me."

Shame bowed his heavy head as he said quietly, "I was a beast to take you."

She wanted to tell him that she had forgiven him; that her life, though perhaps a bit lonely, was much better than it had ever been before. She wanted to thank him for all he had given her since she arrived. But she couldn't find the words she needed, and so they sat in silence until he asked her to marry him and she refused.

Chapter Six

The water made her skirts three times as heavy as they were when dry, and Cecile soon tired of trying to keep their hems out of the dirt as she stalked back to the castle. By the time she climbed the stairs to her room, she was a wet, muddy mess. But she had to laugh as she peeled herself out of the sopping dress and slipped into the bathtub. This had all happened because she had been gathering water lilies at one of the ponds when she reached too far towards the middle and fell completely into the water.

She leaned out of the bathtub and carefully closed her fingers around the lavender soap. There was still algae in her hair which seemed most determined to stay there.

"I certainly hope Beast didn't see that display of coordination!" she said to the bubbles. He always spoke so highly of her that she didn't want him to know some of the ridiculous things she did.

She had stopped by her sewing room in order to pick up her latest project. Her dove had cooed and ruffled its feathers as she told him about her accident. Cecile took that as a reproach for her clumsiness. Now she reached over to the towels and dried her hands, then picked up the bit of tapestry cloth. After examining the work already done, she continued stitching in blood red thread.

She had never spent so much time on such a small needlework. But the rose she was now stitching was special. It was to be a present for Beast. Cecile wasn't sure exactly when she had decided to make a gift for him, but now it was a bit of an obsession with her. The tiniest misplaced stitch infuriated her; the least little imperfection exasperated her. This had to be perfect. As perfect as every real rose Beast had ever given her.

Eventually, the bathwater cooled a bit too much to be comfortable, and Cecile noticed that her toes were beginning to wrinkle in the water. She dried off and looked for her wet gown, but it was nowhere to be found. It made her uneasy when things appeared and disappeared around her, but she was beginning to become accustomed to the unsettling but efficient business of the castle.

She dressed in a simple shift, then pulled the windows open and sat down in front of them to continue with her sewing, hoping her long hair would dry before dinner. She didn't want to have to explain any damp tresses to Beast.

As the rose grew in shape and form beneath her fingers, she let her mind wander to her family. Gerard, as usual, received the majority of her thoughts. His wedding was to take place in just a few days, and she had been watching his progress through her mirror. Cecile desperately wanted to be there for it. He had always told her that when he got married, he wanted her to stand at his side, and sign the register as his witness. And now, he was going to be married without her. At that thought, she had to blink several times before she could see her needle clearly again.

"But it's for the best," she said aloud. "If I wasn't with Beast, Father would never have had the money to establish our family again. If our family were still poor in the country, Gerard wouldn't be able to marry Lavinia. It's much better this way."

Still, it was a depressing thought that she couldn't attend the wedding of her favorite brother.

By dinner time, her project was complete. She had wrapped the small needlepoint in one of her silk scarves and tied it with a velvet hair ribbon. It looked a little odd, but she knew Beast wouldn't mind. She was excited at finally having something to give to him, and found herself impatient for him to arrive. After what seemed a much longer time than usual, the door opened and Beast entered.

"Good evening, Beauty."

"Good evening, Beast."

"Are you all right?" he asked as he sat down.

She laughed wryly. "Oh no! So you saw that little embarrassing episode in my life?"

"Yes—just long enough to see you fall. I was going to come down and help you, but you seemed unharmed."

"Oh, the only harm done was to my pride." She shook her head and laughed. "I was hoping you hadn't seen me."

A smile lit his dark eyes. "Sorry."

"In any case, it's nice to know that you are there to help me should I get myself into any real trouble."

"I will always be there for you."

Cecile reached for his present. "And I want to thank you for that, Beast. I made something for you."

"You did?" His gruff voice was infused with absolute joy.

"Yes." She looked deeply into his eyes and grinned playfully. "Close your eyes and hold out your hands."

He did as he was told, looking a little unsure of himself, and didn't open his eyes until he felt the silk package fall into his hands. He turned it over, then over again, and looked at it curiously. "What is it?"

"Open it."

Beast gently pulled the ribbon loose with his claws, then delicately unfolded the silk scarf. With trembling fingers, he lifted up the tapestry and breathed, "Oh, Beauty."

She leaned forward. "It still isn't as perfect as I wanted it to be…"

Beast was still staring at the rose. "It *is* perfect, Beauty. I'll treasure it. Thank you so much."

"I just wanted to do something for you. You've been so good to me."

He folded up the tapestry and placed it inside his green brocade waistcoat. "I am thankful that I have you to do good things for."

Cecile began making sculptures out of her chocolate mousse, a little hesitant to voice her thoughts. After a few moments of silence, she finally said, "My brother Gerard is getting married."

Beast stiffened, as he always did when she mentioned her family. "That is happy news."

"Yes." She nodded, but kept her eyes on her dessert. "Except that I can't be there."

When she finally dared to look at him, she noticed how pained his expression was. With as cheerful a smile as she could manage, she said, "But I can watch the wedding with my mirror."

Beast raised his head. "Yes. Your mirror will show you anything you wish to see."

An idea occurred to her, and she asked Beast, "Would you let me send him a wedding gift?"

He actually seemed to brighten with that question. "A wedding gift? Of course you may send something!"

"Thank you, Beast! Gerard has always been special to me, and this will make him so happy." She licked the chocolate off her spoon, then remembered her sisters. "Except…my sisters will be angry about that. Josette is married, and Marie is engaged, and I didn't even think about sending them anything!"

"Ah well," Beast said with a snort, "they don't sound as if they deserve anything from you."

"No, I suppose they don't. But I'm glad I'll get to send something to Gerard."

Beast stood up and walked towards the door, motioning for her to follow. She trailed him as he walked down the corridor, wondering where they were going. His strides were so great that she was practically running to keep up with him until he noticed and modified his pace to fit hers. The torches grew brighter as he approached and dimmed again after they passed by.

He led her to one of the locked doors that she could never force open during her adventures while exploring. Taking a key from one of his many pockets, he unlocked the door and leaned all of his weight against it before it opened with a screech. Beast shuddered at the sound, as if his ears were very sensitive to the pitch. He looked back at her and said, "I do not often find a reason to enter this chamber."

As soon as he stepped through the doorway, the torches in the room burst into flame. The light shining off all of the gold and jewels in the room was nearly blinding.

"Oh, Beast, this is splendid!" she exclaimed, walking into the room. Her skirts spilled over the gold coins that were scattered in large piles across the floor. It looked as if the hull of a pirate ship had been cracked open and its contents emptied into the room.

"Do you like it?"

"Oh my." She shook her head. "It's too much!" She had thought only to send a bit of embroidery, perhaps a handkerchief. Something that might have actually been *from her*. Nothing so rich as all that was laid out before her.

"Nothing is too much for you."

"But this isn't what I meant!"

"Do you refuse it?" He sounded hurt.

She looked back at him. He *was* hurt. Beast's generosity was at times almost stifling. But she wasn't going to hurt his feelings over this. Not when he meant it so well. "No. No, I don't refuse it."

Smiling once more, he sat down in a chair by the door. "Then please, choose the wedding gift for your brother."

Beast watched her, resting his shaggy cheek against his large fist, with an amused expression while she dug through the trunks and crawled over the gold and silver coins, looking for an appropriate gift. The room was a virtual mine of odd but interesting things, many of them very old. In one of the trunks she found several bolts of rich fabrics, and in another were fabulous sculptures. There were compasses made of gold, and old clocks and pocket watches, and pieces of splendid jewelry. Whenever Cecile found something that caught her interest, she would hold it up for Beast to see, and he laughed when she decked herself in some of the jewelry she found, making her look very much like a little girl playing in her mother's finery.

When she found anything that she thought might suit Gerard, she placed it against the wall where she could easily see it. Soon she had quite a collection which needed to be sifted through. There were so many things she thought would be perfect for him that it turned out to be very difficult to settle on just one. She knew the adventurer in him would love a compass, and thought how stylish he'd look with one of the pocket watches. There were some snuff boxes that she had set aside merely because she knew how he'd laugh to receive one.

"I've found it!" she called out to Beast at last.

He stood and walked over to her, stepping easily over the large piles of jewels and coins. She was kneeling over a gilded trunk, waiting for him.

"And what have you decided to give your brother?" he asked lightly, leaning over her shoulder.

She held out a large sapphire brooch. The blue stone would bring out the blue in his eyes, and she thought that might be the best thing for his wedding. At least Lavinia would appreciate it.

Beast gazed at the brooch thoughtfully. "That is a lovely gift, Beauty. I'm certain your brother will like it."

Cecile nodded as she placed it on top of the trunk. "Yes, I think he will."

He leaned over and picked up a necklace made of diamonds and placed it next to the brooch. "We'll send this to your brother's bride."

She gasped at the richness of the gift. "Thank you! Lavinia will be thrilled!" She picked up both pieces of jewelry and held them together, turning them over in her hands to watch them sparkle in the light of the torches. "You are far too good to me, my dear Beast."

"Will you marry me?" he asked softly.

Although she knew she should have expected it, she was startled at the question. She blinked several times and glanced around the chamber, looking for some way to end this night without hurting him. There wasn't one. "I can't."

He sighed and turned to leave, his head bowed and his hands clasped behind his back.

"Please wait for me, Beast. I'm not sure how to get back to my room from here."

He laughed quietly. "I'm sorry. Of course I'll lead you back to your room. Leave your gifts on the trunk. I'll see that your brother gets them."

She picked up her skirts and walked to meet him. As he began to pull the heavy door closed, she realized that she hadn't removed the jewelry with which she had been playing. "Wait!"

Beast halted. "What is it?"

"I forgot," she explained as she started to pull the rings off of her fingers.

"Please, Beauty, keep them."

"Keep them?" she repeated in disbelief. She was wearing rings on every finger, several necklaces, some heavy bracelets and bangles, and a net of diamonds on her hair.

"They look much better on you than on the floor," Beast said as he ushered her through the doorway. "Shall I leave it unlocked for you?"

She looked surprised. "Oh, that's not necessary. But thank you."

He closed the door behind him and locked it, then led her down the corridors to her room.

"That's quite a collection you have, Beast," she said as she walked beside him, jangling her bracelets together.

He nodded, but didn't say anything.

"I think if Josette or Marie were here, they'd spend every day in there, just counting the money and appraising the jewels."

Beast gave her a faint smile, but still said nothing.

When they reached her room, he bowed to her in parting and said, "Your gifts will arrive tomorrow."

"Could I please send a note as well? So he knows that I'm all right? My family doesn't know what's become of me, and I know they must wonder."

After a moment's deliberation, he said, "Use the paper on your dressing table, and I will see that he gets it. Good night, Beauty. Sleep well." He handed her a perfect pink rose, which she carefully took from his fingers without touching them.

"Thank you, Beast. Good night."

When he closed the door after her, she didn't see him take the small tapestry out of his pocket and kiss it lovingly. She simply walked to her dressing table to see what kind of paper Beast had left there for her. She had to laugh a little ruefully at the size of it.

She dipped her quill into the inkwell and penned:

Dearest Gerard,

Don't worry about me. I'm safe and well, and even happy. I wish I could be there for your wedding, but know that I am thinking of you. I'm certain that you and Lavinia will be very happy. I remember her as being very sweet. Take care and keep the boys out of trouble. Give my love to everyone, especially Father.

As always, your loving sister, Cecile

There wasn't room enough to write anything else.

Chapter Seven

The music that she had found on her piano the day before was still there, waiting for her and—she was certain—mocking her. Although she loved to play, she had never had any great talent for it. This piece looked as though it would sound absolutely beautiful, but she couldn't get the timing of the melody right. She played it through several times so that at least the notes were right, but felt that she was just going through the motions. The true beauty of the song continued to elude her fingers.

"I'll try again tomorrow," she said as she placed the sheets back into their folder; a capitulation on her part.

Sunlight spilled in through the windows, setting everything aglow. It looked so inviting that she picked up a light cloak and walked outside and into the gardens. The summer air proved to be too warm even for the thin cloak she had taken, so she slipped it from her shoulders and carried it over her arm.

Several fat squirrels and chipmunks scampered out to greet her, now expecting food at her every appearance. Indeed, they had grown much fatter since her arrival. "I'm sorry, babies," she always called them 'babies', though most were full-grown and had babies of their own, "I don't have anything for you today."

They still skipped around her skirts for a few more of her steps until they realized that she truly was unarmed with breadcrumbs and fruits. At that, they dispersed and went back to the trees.

After walking through several of the gardens, she stopped to rest beneath one of the large maple trees that offered so much shade. She spread her cloak out over the grass and sat down, leaning against the tree's gnarled trunk. With a pleasant sigh, she looked up through the leafy branches and said aloud, "One of these days I'm going to wear my old dress out here and climb this tree."

Cecile hadn't climbed a tree since she was six years old and Edmond had dared her to climb to the top of the young oak tree in their courtyard. She smiled at the memory of that. On that day, she had gotten stuck, and both Gerard and Victor had to climb after her and carry her back down, tearing her dress in the process. If she got stuck here, Beast would be the only person who could come to rescue her.

"Perhaps I won't climb it after all," she said quietly, shuddering at the thought of the Beast's hands on her skin.

She leaned back against the tree trunk once more and closed her eyes. Several days ago, she had watched Gerard's wedding. He and Lavinia both wore the jewelry Beast had sent them, which made her feel almost part of the ceremony. Still, not being there had hurt, and that night she cried a good deal more than she had in quite some time.

The warm evening sunlight filtered through the leaves of the old tree, turning her hair red. She toyed with one curl, wondering what her family thought of her letter. It must have surprised them to hear from her after so long, and even more to hear that she was doing well.

At that moment, she noticed a movement on the hillside out of the corner of her eye. She stood to see a dark figure there in the distance. Shading her eyes with her hands, she realized it was Beast. She had never seen him during the day, and often wondered what he did with his time.

"Beast!" she called out, but he didn't hear her. She waited for a long time, hoping that he would look down at her. She didn't quite know what she would do if he did look in her direction, but she wanted him to all the same. He stood there in the glory of the sunset, looking out into the far and away. Cecile watched him for perhaps an hour or more, wishing that he would realize she was there and come down to talk to her. When he finally moved, however, it was to wrap his velvet cape around himself, turn in the opposite direction, and walk away. Feeling a little depressed that he hadn't noticed her, she walked back to the tree and stretched out on her cloak once more. It was nearly night, and she watched the first few stars appear in the darkening sky before going back to the castle.

The candles in the dining room were lit and waiting for her. As soon as she put down her spoon at the end of her meal, Beast walked through the doorway. "So, what did you do today, Beauty?" he asked pleasantly as he sat down.

She rejoiced at the lightness of his voice. "I worked some more on my tapestry, and I played my piano. I took a walk." She looked up at him from beneath her straight, heavy lashes. "I saw you outside today, Beast."

"Where did you see me?" His voice was still pleasant, but with that question it acquired an edge of dark curiosity.

"I was in the garden, by the well. And you were on top of the hill, looking off into the distance. What did you do today?"

"I waited."

His look held such a degree of ferocity that she knew she didn't want to question him further.

"I'm sorry. I didn't mean to frighten you."

"I know." She smiled to reassure him. "I waited a long time for you to look down at me, so that I could wave to you…or something…but you never did."

"No, when I'm out there I don't often look at the castle or its gardens."

"Where were you looking?"

"Away. Simply away." He straightened his shoulders and firmly changed the subject before she had the chance to ask another question. "What did you play on your piano?"

"The music that I found yesterday. I can't seem to get the timing right on it, but I'm going to keep trying. It looks as if it will sound beautiful." She stopped and looked at him. "Beast, how do you know what music I like, and how do you get it for me?"

He smiled at her. "You play music that suits your personality and your moods. When you are happy, you like minuets; and when you are melancholy, you play dirges and requiems. And on those days when I hear a concerto being pounded out, I know that you're angry."

Cecile heaved a playful sigh and rolled her eyes. *A concerto being pounded out.* That was certainly an accurate description of her musical ability. "All right then. How do you get it for me?"

"I get it for you like this." He reached across the table, and by the time his hand was close enough to touch her, there were several sheets of music in it.

She looked startled and her fingers trembled as she accepted the music. "Oh," was all she could say.

He was looking at her with an intensity that made her throat constrict. She swallowed hard. "And what do you do when you aren't 'waiting'?" she asked, reluctant to hear the answer.

"I try to make you happy."

Cecile dropped her gaze to her plate. "Oh."

"Are you happy here?"

"Sometimes."

Beast's whole body seemed to sink and he emitted a sigh that became almost a whimper.

Quickly, Cecile added, "I am not often unhappy."

"You should never be unhappy."

Hanging her head, Cecile sighed, too. She couldn't lie to him. "Thank you for the music."

"Would you like to hear it?"

She looked up, questioning. With a wave of his hand, the air was filled with music so lovely that Cecile felt she could almost see it.

"Beauty, will you marry me?"

"No Beast. I can't."

He got up to leave and the music wrapped itself around her. As Beast dropped the rose onto her plate, she held her hand out to stop him.

"What is it, my Beauty?"

"Beast, sometimes you frighten me, and sometimes you make me angry. But then, sometimes the darkness frightens me, and you do not control the darkness. And sometimes my own foolish thoughts make me angry, and you certainly have nothing to do with that. My piano makes me happy, and you gave me the piano. Books make me happy, and you have given me more books than I could ever have even dreamed of having. My sewing, my paints, and my music make me happy, and you have given me all of that. Unhappiness lurks everywhere, but all of my happiness comes from you."

His expression hadn't changed, nor had he looked at her. "Good night, my Beauty. Sleep well." Without a glance in her direction, he left the room.

Cecile sighed and once more rested her gaze on her plate. It was spilling over with roses.

She pushed open the silver door and stood just inside the doorway, lost in the beauty of what she saw before her. There was a large silver writing desk and behind it, looking as though she were made of silver herself, was the most beautiful woman Cecile had ever seen. She was writing— scratching out something with a pure white quill. Setting down the large plume, she looked up and said very pleasantly, "Then you must be Beauty. Please come inside."

Cecile walked through the room, which looked as though it was wrapped in gossamer, and said, "No, my name is Cecile." Her voice sounded very scratchy and dull in her ears after the melodic voice of the woman.

"My dear, I have seen you through his *eyes, and so you can be only Beauty to me." She smiled and indicated the chair in front of the desk. "Please come here and sit down."*

Cecile did as she was told, noticing when she sat that she was once again in her peasant's clothing. Looking up rather helplessly, she said, "What is this place?"

"It is my place."

"What am I doing here?"

"I must ask you some questions."

"Yes?"

The lady looked at her intently, searching her face and—it seemed to Cecile—her soul as well. Then she asked in her calm, soft voice, "What if you knew him without ever having seen him?"

She blinked and tried to say something, but felt as if she were speaking through gauze. Not a word could escape. She wasn't sure what she was trying to say, anyway.

"What if you had spoken with him without ever having looked upon his face?" the woman continued, relentlessly sweet. "How would you feel towards him if you had never seen him?"

She could feel her heart beating faster as she stared at the flawlessly beautiful face. The woman's eyes were cutting into the deepest part of her soul. Cecile's pulse hammered inside her temples—

So loudly that it woke her. She was in her nightgown, in her bed, and the moon shone silver through the window.

Chapter Eight

The metal scratched her fingers. She was twisting her hairpins together, trying to form a key that might successfully pick some of the locks within the castle. Curiosity had been overwhelming her ever since Beast opened the treasure room for her. Treasure wasn't what she was expecting to find, but all of the castle's locked doors now seemed tremendously inviting.

"Curiosity killed the cat," she kept whispering to herself as she bent the metal over and over again. But that old adage wasn't enough to stop her, and she knew it even as she repeated the phrase; even as she made her way down the corridors with her new key in her hand.

The locks were not giving way as easily as she had hoped, and it wasn't until half a dozen doors had been tried that one finally opened to her. It was the oddest-looking doorway she had ever seen. Instead of the usual doorframe, the oak doors had been set into a large, ornate archway--and looked as if they'd been added as an afterthought. But the audible click of their lock cracking open was as sweet as music.

"Thank you, thank you, thank you!" she breathed. She pushed against the door, but it held fast. Remembering the force that Beast had to use after unlocking the other door, Cecile backed up and ran forward, throwing herself against the heavy wood. "Ow!" But the door creaked open.

The room that was revealed was full of dust and cobwebs. There were windows at the far end, but it looked as if they hadn't been opened in years. Beneath them, at the edge of the vast dance floor, was a massive table, its ornate detail hidden under layers of dust and grime. Large crystal chandeliers, obscured by cobwebs, hung from the ceilings which were painted in murals and supported by large Romanesque columns. At some time—quite a long time ago—this must have been the banquet room.

Cecile looked around in a sort of sad wonder. "This place must have been absolutely beautiful," she said quietly, brushing some of the dust off of the walls as she walked through the room.

The dance floor was made of marble tiles, and perhaps had a pattern at one time. It looked as if the walls might have been pink with gilded trappings, but everything was now a dusky grey. Velvet armchairs, possibly pink, were evenly spaced against the walls. Everything was in its place, as if the room had been cleaned and straightened before being closed for years.

She moved to the middle of the floor and closed her eyes, imagining music and dancers and the celebrations that might have taken place in this room. With a smile, she spun a few circles and then made an elaborate curtsey. Despite its state of disrepair, the room still inspired romantic visions. Yet, whatever wonder this room might have silently witnessed in its past was dead now, never to return.

Her slippers were leaving prints in the dust on the floor and the train of her gown was sweeping up dirt as well. There was no way to pretend she hadn't been here.

"Stealthy, Cecile," she muttered as she shook out her skirts and walked to the door. She placed her makeshift key back into the lock and turned it, but nothing happened. Biting her lip, she tried again. The hairpins spun aimlessly in the large iron lock.

"Great." She felt the tightness of anxiety in her chest. Would Beast discover she had been snooping? Would he be angry? Cecile wasn't afraid of him, but she still didn't want him angry with her. With a guilty sigh, she put the key into her pocket and went on to explore only the rooms that freely opened to her.

There were several corridors that she had never before entered, and they now led her to yet other hallways she had never even seen. Several doors opened, but revealed only empty rooms or cluttered storage areas. A particularly large door in one dark corner opened onto a dark, spiral staircase. Cecile looked up into the gloom, but there was no way of telling how far up the stairs extended. Without a second thought, she began climbing.

Within a few curves of the staircase, Cecile was in almost total blackness. She kept her hands to the wall and continued on for what, in the darkness, seemed like a very long time. Her gown began to weigh on her, becoming tremendously hot. The thought occurred to her that she might remove a few of her petticoats, but she feared tripping on them when she made her way back down. Had she been any less stubborn, she'd have turned around and gone back when the muscles in her legs began to ache. Now, however, she was determined to get to the top just to see what was there.

She heard her head smack the door before she actually felt the pain. Wincing, she placed one hand against her injured forehead and the other against the oak door and pushed. It creaked dreadfully, and the bright sunlight that rushed into the tower was blinding after the darkness. Cecile shielded her eyes and blinked rapidly several times.

The door had opened not to a room, but to a balcony. The peak of the huge round tower was completely open and offered a spectacular view. Even the city could be seen—a lumpy grey line against the horizon. The forest at the foot of the castle did not seem quite so dense when viewed from this height, and Beast's gardens and courtyards were little myriads of color.

'I can see so much from here,' Cecile thought, 'so how is it that we never saw the castle? Or at least this one tower rising out of the forest?' She couldn't reconcile it in her mind, and decided to ask Beast in the evening.

She spent a very long time on the balcony, just to make the climb worthwhile. Although the view was lovely, she didn't think she'd make the effort to see it again any time soon.

After dinner that evening, while carefully neglecting to tell Beast of any explorations into locked banquet halls, Cecile described her day and included the climb to the top of the tower. "But why," she asked, "can't the castle be seen from the city, or even from the road outside the forest?"

"That is how it should be," Beast answered with irritating simplicity.

"What do you mean?" she asked, truly confused. "You should be able to see it. It's so very tall…I don't understand how we could have missed it."

He scratched through the fur above his lace collar and sighed uncomfortably. "Beauty, it is for me that this castle remains…unobtrusive. Think, for a moment, of what would happen should the world know of me, and of my riches here. Both game hunters and treasure hunters are a persistent people, my dearest."

The thought of people coming for her Beast hit her like a blow. It devoured her thinking throughout dinner and was with her when she went to bed. What if some hunter killed him? What if his castle was ransacked? What horrible things could happen if anyone knew he was here? Cecile whispered a fervent prayer that her family had told no one about him—or at least that no one had believed them. But she had terrible dreams that night.

She remained inside the next day as well. Her nightmares had made her reluctant to leave the castle, for fear that it might somehow disappear if she didn't keep it within her sight. It was a foolish fear, but still she couldn't get over it.

As Cecile wandered aimlessly from room to room, she found herself rather hoping to meet Beast somewhere in the castle. Her days were so lonely that she now often wished she could talk to him more often than their evening visits. She knew she had only to ask him to spend more time with her, but somehow the words she needed were never there for her, and so she remained alone.

With the sinking of the sun, she found herself in the painting gallery, watching the moving figures of the masquerade and thinking of the lost splendor of the Beast's ballroom. She stood there for the better part of an hour, staring at that impossible painting. It was only when she realized she was hungry that she walked, almost reluctantly, away from the scene.

After finishing supper early, she stepped out onto the balcony, needing the fresh air after her day indoors. The midnight blue of the sky shone with stars and the air smelled heavily of Beast's roses. Everything was so beautiful that it made her restless. She swirled around lightly, her jeweled skirts spinning around her, and a soft, wonderful waltz filled the air, as if ready to accompany her should she wish to continue her dance.

Caught up in the music and her musings about the ballroom, Cecile began the waltz, allowing her imagination to create a handsome, charming partner for her. She had all but forgotten the Beast's impending visit when she suddenly realized that he was there in front of her, watching her with a smile on his ugly face.

"I'm sorry I startled you," he said when she suddenly stopped. The music disappeared into the air.

"Oh, no. That's quite all right. How long have you been out here?" She felt herself blushing and put her hands up to her cheeks, as if to stop the color from rising.

"Long enough to see that you were enjoying yourself. Did you finish your supper early?"

"Yes. And the stars seemed to call me out here, and the roses made me want to dance." She lowered her gaze to her feet. "I suppose that sounds foolish."

"Of course not, Beauty. Sometimes," he bowed, as though formally ending her waltz, "the roses make me want to dance. Just what is it you were dancing?"

"It's called a waltz."

"Would you like to continue?"

A waltz would mean he'd have to touch her. That couldn't happen. "I don't think I know it well enough to teach anyone. Could we dance something else?" Even as she spoke, her mind raced through the dances she knew. All of them would require her to touch his hands. She bit her lip. There was no polite way out of this.

Beast smiled. "Perhaps I have one to teach you."

With his first movement, a light but pulsating rhythm filled the air. He went through a few steps, then paused while she mimicked him. As they continued on through several measures, Cecile reproached herself for feeling uncomfortable. Beast had chosen a lively, quick-stepped peasant's dance that didn't call for any contact between them. It was such fun that she found herself laughing so hard she could scarcely breathe. Occasionally the steps were too difficult for her to imitate perfectly the first time through, and she stumbled on more than one occasion, but that only made her laugh more. Beast had most certainly been watching her during her times in the courtyards and had seen what ridiculous things she did, for he would definitely not have taught anyone who was truly concerned with lady-like manners a dance such as this one.

After several broad circles and some spins which were quick enough to make her dizzy, she fell, laughing, against the balcony's stone railing. "Oh, we have to stop now! I simply can't go on!"

"Did you enjoy yourself?" Beast inquired with amusement in his voice.

"Yes, very much." She sat on the flat stones of the balcony and leaned against the railing. "Where did you ever learn to do that?"

His brown eyes misted over slightly. "I learned it a very, very long time ago."

"Well, we'll have to try it again sometime…when I've made a full recovery, that is."

She leaned back further against the railing, breathing in deeply and staring up at the stars while Beast stared at her. "Oh, the nights are so pretty here. I missed them for so long. When we lived in the cottage I was always so tired from all of the work that I couldn't stay awake long enough to enjoy them. I'm glad that I have time to feel the nights here. It seems as if the stars are especially bright just over this castle."

Beast stood over her and leaned against the railing, looking over into the gardens. She shifted a little, so that his clothing wouldn't touch her, but if he noticed, he didn't say anything.

"What are your favorite things, Beast?" she asked, still staring into the sky.

He was a little startled. "What do you mean?"

"Your favorite things. Your favorite color, song, book; your favorite place. What are they?"

"Why do you ask?"

She looked at him thoughtfully. "I've come to realize that you are the best friend I've ever had, and yet there are so many basic things that I just don't know about you. You know so much about me, and I would like to know you better."

He smiled again and looked away. "My favorite color is very deep, royal purple."

"Do you like to read or play music, or any of the things that I like to do?"

"I like to read, but these," he flexed his fingers, "were not meant to play music. I sometimes enjoy wandering around the castle and the courtyards just as you do, but I don't believe I get as involved as you do."

She looked at him with a wry grin. "You mean you don't fall into lily ponds."

His laugh was very light. "No, I don't fall into lily ponds."

"And why..." she reached up to stroke some of the soft rose petals that were growing just above her on the railing, "...why are your roses so important to you?"

He looked down over the balcony at all of the flowers climbing towards them. "My roses were important to me because they reminded me that there is true, unselfish beauty in this world. That was before you came here. Now I need only to gaze at your face to restore my faith in beauty."

She watched him very carefully, wondering how to pose her next question. There wasn't a subtle way to ask, so she said simply, "Are there others like you?"

"No," was his solid answer. He turned away and raked his fingers through his shaggy hair. With a deep, even breath, he firmly changed the subject. "Why did you stay inside all day today?"

She lowered her eyes and said, "It was silly."

"Yes?"

Fidgeting, she said, "I was afraid that if I left, you wouldn't be here when I returned." She straightened one curl and watched it spring back. "I said it was silly."

Beast knelt down beside her. "That would never happen."

"I know."

"Why would you even think such a thing?"

"I just...I had terrible nightmares." She looked up into his concerned face and folded her arms tightly across her chest, willing him to let the matter drop. But Cecile knew that he would wait there, staring at her until she told him, so she took a deep breath and blurted out, "I dreamed they killed you."

He blinked a couple of times, as if very surprised, and finally asked, "They?"

"People. They killed you."

"And that was a nightmare?"

"Of course it was!"

His eyes were very serious and his gaze more intense than she had ever felt it before. It seemed to her that he was attempting to stare right into her heart and her mind, searching for something. "Will you marry me?"

"No!" she cried, jumping to her feet and rushing past him into the dining room.

Beast followed her in slowly, standing just behind her.

She didn't know what to do about him anymore. The question that had first inspired fear and loathing upset her now more than ever. She put her hands over her face and tried to calm down. "You are my friend, Beast…my very good friend. But I can't offer you anything more than that! I'm sorry," she said as she sat down at the table.

"Don't be sorry," Beast ordered softly, following her to the table. He stood at her side and said, "It isn't your fault, and I shouldn't ask you for anything. That you consider me even to be your friend is more than I should hope for…and I thank you for your friendship."

He held a rose out to her, his hand trembling. She waited for him to drop it onto her plate as he so often had before, but he didn't. Instead he kept the flower in front of her face, unwilling to release it. She stared at it for what seemed to be a very long time, and still he held it.

"And I am sorry that you find me so repulsive that you cannot even take the rose from my fingers." His voice faltered as he spoke, and the rose fell to the table.

Cecile blushed red with shame. What had she just been thinking? She did find him repulsive…but why? Was she no better than her sisters, who never saw past the appearance? If so, then she was more monster than he.

He was leaving her, his head bowed. Impulsively, Cecile ran behind him and caught his hand in both of hers, causing him to stop in mid-step. He watched, his entire body trembling, as she lifted his hand to her lips. When she kissed him, she felt a shock course through him, and he released a breath that was almost a moan. Their posture didn't change for several moments: she with his hand clenched between hers, he trembling as though he might buckle and fall any second.

Finally, Cecile released his hand and said, "Good night, my Beast."

"Good night, Beauty," he whispered, barely audible. "Sleep well."

His steps sounded especially heavy as he walked away and left her. She stood for a very long time, staring at the doorway. His touch had not harmed her, nor had it sickened her. Without quite knowing why, she sank to the floor and wept.

Chapter Nine

Gradually, the tears slowed, then stopped altogether. She drew her knees up and hugged them to her chest, rocking back and forth. What was going to happen now? The taboo of touching was now broken, so what was going to happen now?

Cecile got back to her feet and returned to the table to retrieve her rose. When he had first offered it to her, it had seemed no different than any of the other roses he had given her before. Their colors had varied, and perhaps one was opened further than another, but they were all just flowers. Beautiful, yes…but just flowers. The rose she now held gently between her fingers was more than beautiful. Its wine-red petals seemed remarkably delicate; its scent especially fragrant. She clutched it to her chest and breathed deeply so as not to start crying again, and walked to her room.

Everything now felt so different to her, although nothing in her bedroom had changed. As she twisted her hair into a long, loose braid, she studied her face in the mirror. Although her skin had finally paled again, she'd not lost all of her freckles. They still sprinkled her nose and fell across her cheeks. Her eyes were a bit red from weeping, but still a pretty aqua shade of green. She watched her fingers as they tied the ribbon at the end of the braid…the same fingers that clumsily played the piano, embroidered ivy leaves into handkerchiefs, and twisted hairpins into keys…those same fingers had just touched Beast's hand and still looked the same as ever.

She shook her head, unable even to voice her thoughts, and went to bed.

A strange man stood before her in the darkened room. He didn't say anything, and his sudden appearance didn't frighten her as it should have. He just stood there and stared at her.

She studied him closely, although she couldn't lift herself out of the bed. He was incredibly beautiful—so much so that a word such as 'handsome' would have seemed a vile understatement. No, this man was not merely handsome. He was very tall, with a tight, muscular build. His brown hair spilled over his shoulders in long, loose curls, framing a long face with a well-chiseled jaw line. His large dark brown eyes were graced with long, thick lashes. He exuded grace and power, but for some reason, behind what must have at one time been a proud countenance, he looked sad. Even when he smiled at her, his full lips parting to reveal perfectly straight, white teeth, he seemed to be melancholy.

His deep brown eyes stared into hers in a way that was unsettling, but not unfriendly. Cecile found her voice and managed to ask, "Who are you?"

He shook his head slowly and turned away. Without a word, the strange man disappeared.

Cecile woke to find herself sitting up in bed, the first streaks of dawn beginning to light the sky.

"Of course it was a dream," she mumbled sleepily. "He was too beautiful to be true."

She settled back into the down pillows and pulled the heavy blankets over her head, feeling very, very empty. Several hours later, she awoke to the light pouring into her room from the French doors.

Taking the glass of cold water that was always waiting on her dressing table when she woke up, she walked out onto the tiny balcony. The morning air was just beginning to warm and she gratefully breathed it in. Noticing that a slight breeze was gently tousling the trees, she loosened the ribbon that bound her hair and shook it out.

"I think I will go outside today," she said to the sunshine. The sun didn't care where she went, but she had to talk to something.

Cecile fell back into bed and pulled a pillow over her face, but wasn't able to stay there long. It was too nice a day to be lazy. She climbed out of bed and opened her wardrobe. From all of the splendid gowns that were there, she chose her old peasant's dress. She dressed as quickly as she could and practically skipped to the dining room. The table was laden with cinnamon breads, fruits, porridge, and pastries. She wondered vaguely what happened to all of the food that she did not eat, for she had never finished what was on the table.

Later, she ran into the library, pulled a book of medieval poetry from one of the shelves, and walked outside. She found herself in one of the far courtyards, standing underneath the large maple tree that had intrigued her earlier. Its branches reached very high up into the sky, drinking in the sun's rays. As the light filtered through, it made strange but wonderful patterns on the grass below: a mosaic of greens. Cecile stepped into the middle of that artwork and looked up into the sturdy branches.

"I wouldn't have to climb that high," she said, staring through the leaves. She looked at her hands. "And Beast would rescue me if I couldn't get back down."

Not quite sure of how to accomplish her goal, she tucked the book into her pocket and hoisted herself up to the first branch. The rough bark scratched her fingers but she barely noticed. As she rose higher and higher, it never occurred to her that she was testing herself; that she truly would let Beast help her. Although she was not consciously thinking of what had happened the night before, she knew now that the Beast's touch would not hurt her, and that knowledge was strangely comforting.

Every few minutes she felt her pocket to make sure that the book was still safely there. About halfway to the top, she stopped climbing and draped herself over one of the branches. *The Song of Roland* was the first epic she turned to, and she leaned against the strong trunk and read aloud—just to hear a voice.

Her family had often laughed at her for crying over what was found in a book, but that had never stopped her from getting involved in the stories. Now she sat weeping over the death of a gallant medieval hero, and loved every minute of it. She skipped over Tristan, Lancelot, and all of the other love stories, although she usually liked to read those first. Instead, she read about all of the heroes of warfare and soldiery, concentrating on all of their brave deeds and avoiding romance. But strangely, when she pictured these characters in her head, they all bore the lovely countenance of the silent man in her dream. She read everything aloud, getting so involved that on several occasions she nearly threw herself out of the tree.

Finally closing the book, she held it tightly to her breast and breathed deeply, "Oh, Beast…thank you for the library!" she exclaimed, still caught up in the magic of the literature. Reading was a passion of hers that no one else had ever understood. But Beast understood. Perhaps he even shared that passion.

Cecile had always lived her life through books. As she was never invited to join her sisters in parties and dances, she had early on found solace in her family's library…and soon preferred it to any other diversion. The only times in her life when she had ever been in love were when she might have fallen for some tragic hero. That, of course, lasted only for as long as the book had pages.

Her stomach growled loudly, reminding her that it was past noon. With a sigh, she put the book back in her pocket, wrapped her arms around the branch she was on, and swung her legs over the side. A little scream escaped her lips as she felt the full force of gravity upon her. The book of poetry fell to the grass below and seemed to her to take an awfully long time to fall.

"All right, find a branch, find a branch," she said, kicking her legs wildly. This was becoming an appalling resemblance to her childhood tree-climbing experiment. Finally, after lowering herself a little further, her feet hit the branch below and she slowly walked her hands down the tree trunk until she was sitting on that lower branch. In this fashion, she managed to make it down to the first branch. It seemed much farther from the ground than it had on the way up. Closing her eyes and taking a deep breath, she swung herself off the last branch and fell to the ground.

The poetry had re-awakened her passion for books. Although it had been over a week since she had been in the library, she found herself there the next afternoon.

An incredibly massive book at the end of one of the shelves caught her eye. It was a complete anthology of Shakespeare's works.

"Fantastic!" she breathed as she eased the large book off of the shelf. Shakespeare had always been her favorite playwright. Cecile carried the heavy volume to one of the large, over-stuffed library chairs and settled down to read. She rifled through the plays, reading her favorite scenes. *Hamlet* made her cry, so she turned to *The Taming of the Shrew* for a laugh. Then, while flipping through the pages, she found something that she had never read before: Shakespeare's sonnets. After reading a few of them she was completely intrigued and had turned the page to some others when she realized that her supper would be ready by this time. Unable to bring herself to leave the book, she took it with her to the dining room.

Cecile sat the book in her lap and leaned it against the table. Then, reading the entire time, she very awkwardly ate her meal.

"Beauty?"

She looked up from the pages of the book a little self-consciously and said, "Oh, good evening, Beast."

He sat down with an amused expression. "Are you enjoying your books?"

"A little too much, I'm afraid. I started reading this in the library and simply couldn't re-shelve it. But I was getting very hungry, so I compromised and brought the book in here."

"I'm very glad that you decided to come. And what is it you find so absorbing?"

Cecile tilted the heavy book so he could see the title.

"Shakespeare," he read with relish.

"Yes. When I learned to read, he was my favorite playwright, so I thought I'd re-read some of my old studies. Then I found these sonnets, and I couldn't put them down."

"They are very good. I have always enjoyed Shakespeare."

Cecile tilted her head and gave him a very intense but curious look. "You like to read Shakespeare?"

"Very much. I always have."

She smiled brightly. "Would you read some to me?"

Beast looked startled. "I? Read to you?"

"Please." With visible effort, she held the book out to him. "Read your favorite sonnet."

He reluctantly took the book from her, holding the heavy volume easily in one hand. After delicately flipping through the pages with his long claws, he read Number One Hundred Sixteen, his rough voice deep and gentle, *"Let me not to the marriage of true minds admit impediments...."*

She closed her eyes and listened to him. His voice expressed so much—feelings and emotions seemed to flow from him. It was as if he were pouring his entire soul into those fourteen lines. She didn't realize she was crying until she felt the tear roll off of her cheek.

He looked up at her when he finished and leaned forward. "Beauty, have I upset you?"

"No," she said, brushing the tears away with her fingers. "It was beautiful."

"Thank you."

"How do you do that?"

"Do what, Beauty?"

She shrugged and looked around the room, groping for the words she wanted, but couldn't find them. Finally, she asked, "How do you make the lines *feel*? How do you do that?"

Beast's eyes seemed to sink right through her. "I simply envision something very special to me."

Cecile couldn't look away from him. "Oh."

"Here," he said, easily handing the book across the table to her, "now you read your favorite."

She did not yet have a favorite, but there had been one that had struck her, and she searched through the pages until she found Number Ninety-Four. *"They that have the power to hurt, and will do none...."*

As she finished, he bared his teeth in a smile. "You have a lovely reading voice."

"Not half so lovely as yours," she said as she attempted to hand the book back to him. He reached across the table and took it from her with a questioning glance. "Please read some more to me."

"Do you enjoy it so much?"

Cecile nodded as she cleared the table in front of her and leaned against it. "Yes, I do. Will you do it for me?"

"What shall I read?"

"Anything you want. Maybe some more of the sonnets?"

He nodded, caressing the book as he could not caress her. "Whatever you wish." And he read to her for the rest of the evening.

Chapter Ten

"Beast, guess what today is." She scraped her spoon around on her plate, playing with what was left of her dinner.

He gave her a questioning glance. "I don't know. Is today something special?"

"In the grand scheme of things, probably not." She grinned. "But it is my birthday."

His eyes widened. "Why didn't you tell me earlier so I might have done something for you?"

She laughed softly. "Oh, Beast. I didn't even know until today. It seems that there's no way to keep track of time here, but I happened to check on my family today, and they were talking about it. Edmond said he hoped I was enjoying myself. I was rather surprised to hear it was my birthday. I hadn't realized so much time had passed."

Beast tugged on the lace at the cuffs of his satin blouse. "Happy birthday, Beauty. Is there anything that I might do for you?"

With a playful sigh, she said, "Beast, I didn't tell you just so you'd give me something. Besides, you give me presents practically every day. What more could I ask for just because it's my birthday? I would feel selfish."

"Please let me do something for you."

"If it will make you happy."

"It will make me very happy," he said, an intense and almost frightening passion behind his voice.

Cecile swallowed with difficulty, her throat feeling suddenly very constricted. Why did that sound in his voice always make her feel so helpless and flustered? She glanced around the room, but nothing came to mind. With a shrug she said, "I don't know what to ask for, Beast. I have practically everything I could ever think to wish for."

"Then there is nothing that I could do for you?" He sounded very disappointed.

"You do everything for me." She began to unconsciously tie knots in her napkin. "You make me happy, Beast. That is the best present I could ever have."

He smiled almost shyly. "Thank you, my Beauty. But still I must give you a gift."

In a great swirl of blue smoke, a beautifully wrapped box appeared beside Cecile's chair. She bent down to pick it up and placed it on the table, surprised at how heavy it was. Beast motioned excitedly for her to unwrap it, so she carefully tore at the paper.

Inside the package was a water-globe filled with colorful glitter. There were figures inside of the globe as well: dancers dressed for a masquerade. Cecile took it into her hands gingerly and turned the key at its base. A piece of music that Beast had once given her for her piano floated out as the masqueraders began to dance inside the globe. The glitter swirled around them in the water, creating a little dream world.

"It's wonderful, Beast," she breathed, watching it with rapt attention. This couldn't be a coincidence. He must have known how often she stood in the gallery to watch the painting of the masquerade. Now she could have this scene in her bedroom, with the music included. "Thank you."

"You're welcome, my Beauty."

She placed the globe on the table as the music slowed and died away. "This is the most fantastic birthday present I've ever been given. Why do you do so much for me?"

"Because I…I enjoy seeing you happy." He stared at her for long moments, watching her every movement. She noticed that he did that quite often, but it no longer bothered her. She merely folded the wrapping paper as if unaware of his eyes on her.

"Beauty," he finally said, "why did you never marry? Surely there were proposals enough."

She wondered what had placed that question in his thoughts. Perhaps the mention of her birthday brought with it the realization that at her age she should have at least been betrothed by now. Beast often asked questions that should not be asked in polite society. But then, the two of them in this lonely castle did not exactly constitute a 'polite society', so what did it matter?

"Proposals there were, but love there was not."

"What do you mean, 'love'?" Beast inquired.

Cecile pushed her plate away. "I mean that I didn't love the men who proposed, and they didn't love me."

"Were they from low stations?"

She felt just a tinge of insult. "No, they weren't, but I don't see what that has to do with it. I would have married a blacksmith if I'd loved him. My sisters turned down many men because they weren't as important as Josette and Marie thought their husbands should be, and when we were poor, even those men wouldn't take them. And when they became rich again, they suddenly had suitors again. There was no love in those proposals, either. I didn't want anything like that. I didn't want my marriage to be a business proposition. I wanted to marry for love."

"Beauty," Beast began, a little startled at her outburst, "many people who don't love each other do marry. Sometimes they learn love afterwards."

"Yes, I know, and sometimes they don't." She drank what was left of her wine. "The dangerous thing about books is that they can give you a very romanticized view of love, and I'm just the fool to believe in it. I wanted what my heroes and heroines had. I wanted to *be* in love; to be silly and romantic and passionate. Just to feel it. My father, however, wanted me to marry. I think he was getting impatient…afraid I'd never choose someone." She gave Beast a brief, sad smile. "Now he doesn't have to worry about it anymore."

"It is very noble of you not to sacrifice your wishes too soon."

She spoke very quietly, her voice almost a whisper. "And now I will never fall in love."

Beast leaned forward over the table. "Do you love me, Beauty? Will you marry me?"

Cecile sighed, trying not to notice the tremendous passion in his voice. "You are my best friend. I like you very much, my dear Beast."

Some of the light behind his eyes flickered and died. "Good night, Beauty. Happy birthday." The rose fell lightly in front of her.

It became increasingly difficult for Cecile to reject Beast's proposals. She realized too late that, because of one conversation, she was no longer just saying, '*I will not marry you*', she was saying '*I do not love you*'. As if it were possible, Beast began to look sadder and sadder with every rejection.

But why was it infinitely harder to say 'I don't love you'? Although she pitied him, it was not difficult to tell him she would not marry him. So why should love be so much harder to deny him?

She was breaking his heart. She knew that—had always known it. She found that knowledge to be absolutely tortuous.

"Beauty, will you marry me?"

Sometimes she wanted to stand up and scream, "I am not Beauty! My name is Cecile! I can't be what you want me to be. I can't do what you want me to do. Please stop asking me!"

And then there were times when she felt that her own heart was breaking. She felt so sorry for him, and so guilty at hurting the one person who depended on her alone for happiness. But *yes* was something she would never say to him. Yet, he continued to call her Beauty. He continued to care for her and watch over her. It didn't seem quite fair.

He loved her. She was aware of that with every longing look towards her, with every sigh, with every question, and with every rose. But she could not return his love. She missed him during the day and waited impatiently for the hour of his visit. She searched for things during the day that might interest him to hear in the evening. If he quoted a book or an author during dinner, she was sure to find it in the library the next day and read it. She watched operas through her mirror and shared the plots with him, describing sets and costumes in great detail, just to see his eyes sparkle. He was strong and compassionate and caring, and it seemed that there was something in him that was as lovely as his appearance was horrible. The roughness of his voice was something she found to be beautiful, and she thought his eyes were the deepest and most luminous she had ever seen. She rejoiced when he was happy, and felt sadness when he was sad, but, of course, that was not love. It couldn't be. Not for Beast.

Chapter Eleven

The stone garden wall was so high that she couldn't quite see over it. Through the rusted bars of the large iron gate, Cecile could see only tall green hedges, but that only served to heighten her curiosity. She'd often wondered what might be behind those walls, but had never been so determined to find out as she was today.

She tried both pushing and pulling against the gate, to no avail. "Key," she whispered to herself, "there must be a key for this." She kicked around at the stones near her feet, kicking them harder and harder as time went by and no key appeared. When she finally sent one poor stone sailing at the expense of her toes, she had to laugh at herself.

"Cecile, you're so accustomed to having your every wish granted that you've become a real brat!"

After tugging on the gate one last time, she turned and walked back towards the castle, wiping the rust stains from her hands. The setting sun indicated that it was nearly time for her supper. So, although she did not feel the least bit hungry, she went inside, deciding that she would ask Beast about the garden.

She sat at the dining room table and ate a little of everything just out of politeness. But, as soon as politeness allowed, she opened the glass doors and stepped out onto the large balcony. The air was deliciously cool against her skin, and she took the combs out of her hair and shook it loose to let it blow freely about her face.

The courtyards looked wondrous in the twilight. White statues could be made out against the background of the green grass and the dark sky, dotting the landscape like distant ghosts. She could see some of the fountains still spouting their waters which looked purple in the fading light. Beast's roses filled the night air with their sweet, heavy perfume. Looking over the railing, she saw their deep red petals nodding in the breeze. Cecile breathed in their scent, feeling almost content. She walked back and forth along the railing, trailing her hand over the stone and rose petals.

She was just thinking how the rough stone and smooth petals reminded her of Beast's voice when he stepped onto the balcony and let the lace curtains fall together behind him.

"Good evening, Beauty. How long have you been outside tonight?"

She continued her promenade. "Quite a while. I didn't eat very much tonight."

He ventured out a little further. "Was everything to your liking?"

"Yes, Beast. Everything is always delicious. I just wasn't very hungry tonight. I came in this evening more for your company than for supper."

He smiled, very pleased. "Then were you outside today?"

"For most of the day, actually. It has been very nice outside lately."

"Yes. It's been quite lovely."

"I walked quite a long way out today. I went down to—Ouch!" she cried as she caught her hand on a thorn.

In an instant, Beast was beside her. "Beauty, what happened? Are you hurt?"

"Just a little scrape," she said lightly, although it stung so sharply that it made her eyes water. She held her hand out for him to see, the wounded palm turned up. "The roses you give me never have thorns, so I guess I've just become careless."

"Oh, I'm so sorry, my Beauty." He gently took hold of her hand in both of his. A trickle of blood welled up from her palm. With surpassing tenderness, he bent his rough head and kissed the slight wound.

She gasped at the touch and he quickly released her hand and stepped back.

His eyes were filled with something very close to terror. "I'm sorry." He turned and began to walk away from her very quickly.

She watched him leave her, her breathing shallow and her thoughts in an uproar. As Beast placed his hand against the cold glass of the doors, she found her voice and called after him, "It's all right. Please don't go."

"Don't go?" he asked as though he couldn't believe that he'd heard her correctly.

"Don't go away. Please." She took a few steps towards him. "Please stay and keep me company. Please."

He finally turned to face her again and nodded slowly.

"Good." She smiled, but her bottom lip trembled. Then, although she suddenly felt incredibly warm, she said, "Let's go inside. It's getting rather chilly out here."

He followed her in and sat down opposite her at the table, but neither one of them spoke for quite some time. Beast stared at his hands, which were folded in his lap, and sat still as a statue. Cecile, however, could not keep still at all. She smoothed her hair back, folded and re-folded her napkin, straightened the ropes of pearls on her bodice, and twisted her rings around her fingers. Gripping her goblet tightly, she drank all that was left in it, trying to steady herself. Her hand seemed to burn where his lips had touched her, but it felt so wonderful that she could hardly breathe.

After what seemed to be hours of uninterrupted silence, she remembered that she had wanted to ask about the locked garden. Greatly relieved at finally having something to say, she asked, "Beast, have you ever been inside the locked garden?"

"It is locked for a reason." He still wasn't meeting her eyes.

"Oh."

With a heavy sigh he reached into one of his many pockets and removed a key. After staring at it for a moment, he held it out to her. "This is the key. The gate is rusted and you will have to turn this key very roughly in order to gain entrance."

She took the key from him and he withdrew his hands. "Why do you give me this?"

"I can deny you nothing." He looked into her eyes at last. "But do not wander very far within its walls. I would not want anything to happen to you."

"Is it dangerous?" she asked, half frightened and half intrigued.

"If you got lost, perhaps."

"Then should I not go inside?"

"You may go where you wish. I would not allow you to remain lost for long."

She managed a smile for him once more. "What is inside those walls?"

"A labyrinth."

"Truly? Oh, that sounds fantastic!"

"Please be careful."

"Don't worry. I'll take the advice of Ariadne and bring along some thread. That way I'll know how to find my way out." She laughed nervously, wondering briefly when her breathing would return to normal.

Beast was still sitting rather hunched over in his chair, looking ashamed of himself. "Will you marry me?"

Cecile could barely hear him, but she knew what he had said. She dropped her gaze and sighed, then shook her head slowly.

He gave her a deep red rose, then walked silently from the room, leaving her holding the gate key in her still-burning hand.

Late the next morning, Cecile was at the locked garden armed with the large brass key. As Beast had said, the gate was very hard to unlock, and she managed it only after a struggle. It finally swung open with a mighty shriek of indignation at being bothered after such a long rest. Beyond the wall were vast hedges, so tall that she could not see over them. She pulled the spool of thread out of her pocket—for she had indeed brought it with her—tied the end around one of the bars on the rusty gate and started through.

She was lost almost instantly because she was paying attention more to the sights than to which way she was going. The locked garden was a wondrous place. At the first dead-end corner Cecile found a small fountain which contained several tiny goldfish. In several places, she turned the corner to find a wall of honey-suckle or grapevines looming up in front of her. At other dead-ends, she found statues or marble garden benches. She found so many of these things and had to turn around so many times that she would have been hopelessly lost if not for her thread.

Beast's request was forgotten as she went deep into the middle of the maze to discover the largest of the fountains in the labyrinth. A beautiful stone mermaid was rising up on a stone wave, her hands lifted to the sky and her hair spread out like a fan behind her. On every side of her the fountain spewed colored waters high into the air, surrounding the mermaid with a watery rainbow.

"Oh, how beautiful," Cecile exclaimed, holding her hand out to let the cold water splash against her skin.

Many hours later, tired and hungry, Cecile stopped and looked around her. She could see the way out; that was easy. The white thread shone brightly in the moonlight, ready to help her should she need it. But it seemed like such a long way to the castle...and her feet hurt from so much walking. Her visit with Beast was already long over. She hoped he hadn't missed her too much. She hadn't missed him at the time—this garden held too many wonders for her mind to stray from it—but now she rather wished she had heard his voice on this evening.

As she thought about it, she realized that she wished he had been here with her this day. It would have been nice to have shared all she'd discovered with Beast. Maybe some day he would come out with her.... Maybe some day she would find her voice to ask him.

There was a marble garden bench a couple of paces from her that was beginning to look very inviting. After tying off her thread around one leg of the bench, she called out, "Beast! I'm not lost! Don't worry!" She looked around, wondering if he had heard her and half expecting an answer. When no sound came, she lay down. The night air was very warm, so she did not regret being without her blankets or quilts. Within minutes, she was asleep.

Several hours later, the Beast stood over the bench, looking down at her longingly. "Oh, my poor Beauty—you are much too close to my hunting grounds. You should sleep in the room I have given you." He knelt beside her sleeping form. "I missed your company this evening. I can only hope that you missed mine as well. Please come to dinner tomorrow evening, for as beautiful as you are by moonlight, I would like to see you sitting close to me—to feel your gaze and the friendship it holds."

He gently brought a copper curl to his lips, then placed a white rose against her hair. "Good night, my Beauty and my love. Sleep well," he said as he sat down on the grass and rested his head against the cool marble of the bench, watching over her as she slept.

Chapter Twelve

The silver lady waited patiently for her to enter the parlor, smiling invitingly. As Cecile walked inside, the lady beckoned her to stand in front of the silver writing desk. A man was waiting for her, his back turned. Yet, even before he turned to face her, she knew who it was. That tall, muscular build and soft brown hair belonged to the beautiful man she had once dreamed about.

He smiled as he met her eyes; a smile pleasant and friendly, yet sad. There was something in that smile, and in those eyes, that she knew, and yet she couldn't think why she should know them. With a fluid motion conveying such grace and power that she was helpless to resist, he took her by the arms, bent his head, and kissed her.

She didn't pull back, but she also didn't return the kiss. Instead, she stood in the midst of this embrace bewildered and silent. When he finally drew away from her, she was startled to see not the man, but Beast. Suddenly unafraid, she threw herself into his arms and kissed him passionately, her mouth open to those black lips, those sharp teeth...her hands fisted in the coarse fur that was there in the place of the other man's soft hair. His arms closed around her, the dangerous claws piercing through the delicate fabric of her gown. Such a warm, sweet, passionate kiss...

With a gasp, Cecile sat up in her bed, shaking terribly. She ripped the blankets off of her and furiously kicked them off of the bed, as if there was something poisonous within their fibers. In a panic, she spun around, half-expecting to find Beast there in her room. But, of course, the room was empty save for her. She caught sight of herself in the mirror, standing in her nightgown amidst the disheveled bed, sweating and gasping as if she'd run a marathon.

"Why would I have dreamed that?" she practically shouted. She looked down at the mattress and jumped off of the bed, as though it was the source of her troubled thoughts.

Shuddering, she pulled a quilt out of her trunk and stalked down the corridors and stairs to the library, intent on reading comedies until morning.

But she couldn't concentrate on anything she took off the shelves, and nothing took her mind off of her unsettling dream. She could still feel the warmth of those arms around her, and the fact that her body rejoiced in that warmth made her mind recoil all the more.

Cecile sat back and stared at the flames in the fireplace. Why would she have dreamed such a thing? It didn't even make sense. And what was this silver lady meant to be? Before coming to the castle, Cecile had never dreamed about the lady. She pulled the quilt closer around her shoulders and shuddered, too upset even to cry.

The dawn came, and turned to day while Cecile remained in the library, in her nightgown. Eventually, she fell asleep in the chair, too exhausted to dream. The dining room table was set for lunch before she finally returned to her room and dressed. As she sat at the table, she imagined Beast coming in to sit across from her after dinner. He would smile, of course. He would have a rose for her. Perhaps he would even brush his fingers against hers in one of those tentative touches he sometimes dared to make. At that thought, she buried her face in her hands.

"No, no, no. I can't face him today. I'll apologize tomorrow, but tonight I just can't look at him."

She knew such a decision would hurt his feelings, but her stomach clenched every time she thought of changing her mind. And so after a listless day in which nothing was accomplished, she filled a plate and goblet, and took both to her bedroom, not even risking the chance that Beast might arrive early.

The next morning, however, dawned bright and peaceful. Cecile was able to look at the entire preceding day as one long nightmare, and one which she was glad was over. She did feel badly about neglecting Beast, though, and by evening had decided on her apology.

After dinner, she dragged the heavy chairs from the table and placed them in front of the fireplace so that they faced each other. She placed a book on one velvet seat, then sat in the chair opposite, her head bowed and her fingers fidgeting with her dress.

Beast appeared in a few moments and stood just inside the doorway, casting a furtive glance into the room. "Beauty, do you wish to see me this evening?" He asked it so hesitantly that it wrenched her heart.

"More than anything else."

At that he entered, but with a more halting step than usual. When he realized what she had done with the chairs, he stopped short and asked, "What is this?"

"A new arrangement for tonight."

"And the book?" he asked with amusement in his voice.

"I thought perhaps you could read to me again."

He looked at the title and then back to her. "Don Quixote?"

"One of the very best."

He picked up the book and flipped through the pages gently, then shut it. "And are you certain you want me sitting so close to you?"

"Of course." She bit her lip and sighed heavily. "Beast, I'm very sorry about yesterday. Please understand that it had nothing to do with anything you did. I just…I just wasn't feeling myself. That's all."

"Are you well?"

"Yes. I'm fine."

"Then that is all that matters to me." He smiled at her and sat down. "Where should I start?"

She felt relief flood through her and smiled back at him. "From the bookmark, if you like. Or from the beginning. I'll be happy just listening to your voice tonight."

He sat back and opened the volume at the silk bookmark. After reading two chapters with such vigor and imagination that Cecile found herself clapping her hands and laughing, he closed the book and looked at her with a smile shining through his luminous brown eyes. "Well now, did you enjoy that?"

"Yes, Beast! You're better than any story-teller I've ever heard!"

"I'm glad that I can do something for you."

"You do everything for me." She leaned over and placed her hand over his, feeling him quiver at the touch. "Is it all right if I ask you to read to me every once in a while?"

"I will do anything you wish," he said in a husky and strangely hollow voice.

She didn't doubt that for a second. "I hope that you enjoyed reading this as much as I enjoyed listening," she said as she removed her hand from his.

Beast seemed suddenly able to breathe again and said, "I enjoy doing whatever makes you happy. It has been a long time since I last read this. I did like reading it again."

"How many of the books in the library have you read?" she asked. "Perhaps I could choose something new for you next time."

He shook his head. "Nothing in there is new to me. Choose whatever you like, my dear."

Her mind raced through the shelves in the library. There were thousands upon thousands of books in that room. More books, she was certain, than she could read in a lifetime. How could nothing in there be new to him?

"Have you read all of them?"

"Yes."

"Every single one?"

He laughed lightly at her persistence. "Yes, I have read every single one."

"Beast," she began quietly, very unsure of herself, "sometimes, such as when you read in such amusing tones, you seem to be very young. But there are times when you seem to me to be much older…and if you have been here long enough to have read everything in the library…"

She trailed off but he finished her thought. "Then yes, I am very old."

Cecile looked at him closely, but how could one place age on such a countenance? She knew that he walked with firm and measured steps, that his voice was full and steady. His eyes were full of life and intelligence. There was nothing about him that would ever have caused her to believe that he was 'very old'.

"How long have you been here?"

Beast drifted his long fingers over the leather binding of the book thoughtfully. "I don't quite remember. Perhaps a century. Perhaps longer."

"A century?" she whispered, her voice cracking.

He looked at her awed and slightly horrified face and said softly, "Please, my dear, do not let it worry you."

But she barely heard him. She had still not grasped that sense of time. "But a century?"

"Yes."

Her breath caught in her throat and she lowered her gaze to her lap. "Have you been alone for all of that time?"

"Yes, for all of that time."

A wave of nausea crashed over her, and she closed her eyes and turned away. Alone for all of that time. It was inconceivable. She suddenly felt angry with herself for even feeling lonely simply because she had no company during the day. She had never been alone. But she had been his only companion for years, and yet she would abandon him over something as pointless as a stupid dream. Until that moment, she hadn't realized the depth of his dependence on her. Cecile silently vowed never to miss another visit with him.

After watching her in silence for many moments, Beast gave the book to her. "Beauty?" he ventured softly.

She looked up as if surprised to hear him, her eyes wide and vacant, her thoughts tripping through a century of the castle. When he didn't say anything, she gazed down at the book and rubbed her hand over it. The leather cover felt smooth against her fingertips, and was still warm from Beast's hands. She hugged it tightly and brushed her cheek against the back cover.

"Beauty, will you marry me?"

She raised her eyes to meet his and slowly shook her head. "I can't, Beast." Her refusal was more anguished than his acceptance of that refusal had ever been.

He held a rose out to her and she took it from him with trembling fingers. Cecile gripped the flower tightly; almost wishing it had thorns.

"Please, Beauty, don't trouble yourself with this. Now that you are here, I am happy. I would spend ten centuries alone if at the end of them I could be with you."

"You're sweet," she said absently, barely hearing him.

"No. I mean what I say." He shook his head, at a loss for anything to do. "Good night, Beauty. Sleep well."

"Good night, Beast. And I'm sorry. I'm very, very sorry for having missed dinner with you last night. Please believe me when I tell you that I felt the absence as much as you did."

"Thank you."

She watched him leave in silence. A century. He had been completely alone for a century. Perhaps longer. She looked at the familiar room around her and felt its space for the first time. This place had been his lonely domain for one hundred years. How many times might he have walked through these rooms and down the corridors with only the echoing of his own footsteps to accompany him? She stood up and walked up the stairs to her rooms, the loneliness of a century surrounding her.

Chapter Thirteen

After wandering through the many winding corridors, she finally found the strange doorway that led to the decrepit banquet room. Cecile walked inside and kicked at the dust on the floor, building up her courage. She had worn her old dress and had brought with her the brooms, mops, sponges, and buckets that she had scrounged from every odd corner in the castle. Old servants' quarters and storage areas had been raided of their contents, which were now stacked in the center of filthy dance floor.

For some time now Cecile had been determined to do something special—something monumental—for Beast. She couldn't give him that which he most wanted, but she decided she *would* grant him one thing she had previously denied him. Now, as she looked around the room, she began to wonder if her stubborn determination might be too much for her ability.

"We'll soon find out," she said aloud, walking to the massive windows. She hefted the broom and with a loud yell began beating the velvet drapes, knocking the dust out of the fibers.

A shower of dust immediately descended upon her head, coating her braided hair and getting into her eyes. "Ew, yuck!" she cried, then sneezed. With a laugh she gazed defiantly at the curtains and said, "If I could clean out a little cottage that had been left to the squirrels and mice for years, I can clean you, too!"

She beat the curtains until she was breathless, and yet dust continued to fly from them for quite some time. Eventually, she had to stand on a chair and use a long handled broom to reach the valance, for the windows were easily twice as tall as she was. By the time the drapes had been returned to a pretty salmon shade of pink, the floor beneath them was piled with dust and lint. Cecile swept it away, then pulled the curtains back and bound them tightly with their sashes, leaving the windows free of them.

A row of buckets stood behind her, each full of water. One by one, she emptied each bucket against the window panes, managing to splash herself with almost as much water as hit the glass. Then she gathered the buckets and took them out to fill them once more. Her shoulders were already beginning to ache, but just imagining how pretty the banquet room was going to look once she finished kept her cheerful. With the stringy little mop she found, she scrubbed top rows of panes until they shone clear, then jumped off of the chair and continued scrubbing down to the bottom. The remaining buckets of clean water were then splashed against the windows, rinsing away any trace of dirt…and creating an even larger pond of mud on the floors beneath. Cecile resolved to leave the floor for last. It would certainly get worse before she had finished.

She stepped out gratefully for lunch, stretching out over the arms of her chair in a most unlady-like manner as she ate. Her body hadn't ached like this since she'd first learned to do housework in the little cottage. And the little farmhouse hadn't been quite the project that this banquet room was going to be. True, the farm had been neglected for years, but the entire house could have fit neatly in the banquet room, and in the house she'd had help from four men. But returning some of the splendor to that wonderful room was going to be far more satisfying than clearing the cobwebs out of a dingy little cottage.

On her return, she began work on the walls, once more setting a line of buckets behind her. Perched precariously on a high-backed chair, she wondered if perhaps she was mad for not asking Beast to give this room to her. She knew she had only to ask, and the entire room would be sparkling clean, the chandeliers glowing, the enormous table laden with food. And yet, if she did that, this would merely be another thing Beast had done for her...not something she was doing for him.

Within a few hours, the bottom half of the walls had gone from a horrid dusky grey to a soft, delicate shade of pink with gilded trappings. There was no possible way for Cecile to reach the top portion of the walls, no matter how many chairs she stood on. The ceilings of the room were as high as any in a cathedral, and so she had to be content with cleaning only what she could reach. This left an odd, two-toned look to the room, but it couldn't be helped.

There was still the floor and the table left to be done when she decided to call it a day. Dinner was only two short hours away, and there was no chance she was going to let Beast see her looking like a dusty scullery maid. She stacked up all of her cleaning equipment, closed the curtains over the window, and carefully shut the door behind her.

The bath water was ready as soon as she entered her room. She quickly disrobed and slipped past the bubbles into the hot water. The stiffened muscles in her back and neck gradually relaxed and left her feeling so extraordinarily tired that she very nearly fell asleep. Rousing herself, she scrubbed her hair and skin until every bit of dirt had been removed. Confident that she now smelled of lavender soap rather than dust, she climbed out of the porcelain tub and wrapped herself in towels before sitting at her dressing table.

The face that reflected back in the mirror was tired and flushed, but clean. Her hair was still damp, and the curls that were usually calm and soft had gone quite wild. She carefully placed several pins and managed to gather most of the curls together with a ribbon at the back of her neck. After donning her simplest gown and a few pieces of jewelry, she deemed herself ready to see Beast.

Dinner left her feeling even sleepier. Was it possible that she'd done so little work since she'd been here that one day of it left her incapacitated? After several embarrassingly wide yawns, she decided to wait for Beast on the balcony where the cool air might serve to rouse her. But she drifted off and didn't wake until she felt a warm hand on her hair.

"Beauty? Beauty, are you all right?" Beast was kneeling beside her, something between concern and amusement in his voice.

Cecile gave him a sleepy smile and sat up, rubbing her cheek. She could feel the marks left by the post against which she had fallen asleep. "I'm sorry, Beast. I guess I'm a little tired tonight."

"Are you ill?"

"No, I'm all right. Just tired." She held her hand out to him and he helped her to her feet.

"What did you do today?"

"I started on a new project. There's quite a lot to it, which is why I'm so tired."

"Ahh…did you enjoy yourself?"

"Not as much as I'm going to once it's finished."

Beast looked deep into her eyes, as if searching for something. "Are you *certain* you're all right?"

"Yes, Beast. I promise you that I'm fine." She smiled at him, thinking how astounded he'd be to know what she had really been doing. "I'm just a little tired."

"Then you should go to bed."

Her smile disappeared. "But we haven't had time to talk," she said, more than a little hurt.

He stepped away from her, backing into the railing. "You would rather talk to me?"

"You know I would."

He grinned and folded his arms across his broad chest. "That is wonderful to hear. But still, you should get some sleep tonight. Then perhaps you will be better prepared to talk tomorrow."

After stifling another yawn, she laughed and nodded. "Yes, you're right. I'll—Oh look!" She pointed into the blackness as a star fell across the sky.

Beast leaned against the edge of the balcony. "They are always quite beautiful, aren't they? Even when they fall."

"I hadn't ever seen one fall before tonight. You're supposed to make a wish, aren't you?"

"Yes. I suppose you are."

Cecile closed her eyes and whispered her wish, then looked up to find Beast watching her. "Are you going to wish for anything?"

He obediently closed his eyes and whispered, his voice rumbling deep within his chest. "And now," he said as he looked at her again, "you go to bed and to sleep."

"What did you wish for?"

"You aren't supposed to tell." Beast pushed the glass doors open and followed her back into the dining room. "Will you marry me?"

"I can't."

He handed her the rose and said in a very heavy voice, "Then falling stars are nothing remarkable."

Cecile clutched his hand, the rose caught between their palms, and held him there for a long moment. They stood, staring at each other, with worlds of questions in that stare. Finally, Beast reached out with his free hand and stroked her cheek, a melancholy smile crossing his black lips. "Good night, Beauty. Rest well, and talk to me tomorrow."

The banquet table bore the brunt of her frustrations the next morning. As she scrubbed, she heard Beast's voice in her head. She hated having to hurt him every night. No matter how pleasant their visit might have been, or how much they might have enjoyed each other's company, it always came down to that. Why couldn't he just accept it and stop asking?

Her furious scrubbing had revealed a magnificently carved cherry-finished tabletop before she even realized it. Gold roses were engraved along the edges, their leafy vines continuing down the table legs. Once Cecile stopped brooding long enough to notice the beauty she had uncovered, she stepped back to admire the work. It must have taken some craftsman—or a team of craftsmen—months to complete the entire work.

The table's matching chairs were not to be found, so she cleaned two of the velvet armchairs and placed them at either end of the table. Her next step was to clean the room's marble columns as high as she could reach, once again leaving a two-toned effect.

The ceiling was so high that she could not hope to reach the chandeliers, which were covered in dust and cobwebs. She found the chain that at one time would have lowered them, but they were so massive that she knew she couldn't do it by herself. Perhaps when Beast walked in, the candles would flare up, burning quite a bit of the monstrous apparatus off of the crystal. With the chandeliers out of her reach, this left only the floors to be done.

Starting with a wide stable broom, Cecile swept the dirt and dust into large piles which she then carted outside. A smaller straw broom gathered the finer bits of dust and lint, which she emptied into a basket to be carried out later. Then the buckets came into play again as she emptied them out and mopped up the water. The pink marble gave way to mosaic tiles as she neared the center of the vast floor. Royal blue, gold, and pink were arranged in fantastic patterns. It seemed as if the entire floor were some kind of puzzle. As she got on her hands and knees and polished the tiles with her handful of rags, she realized that if she looked very closely, creatures and scenes emerged from the colors: dragons, unicorns, sea serpents, winged lions. She examined them intently, marveling at the detail, but when she stood up she lost the patterns and found them again only after kneeling down and searching again.

By late afternoon, the floor was so clean that the tiles reflected. Cecile stood back and proudly examined her work. The place was wondrous. She went through once more and wiped her dusting rag over everything again, assuring herself that nothing was left to be done.

She returned to her room and collapsed on the bed, napping for nearly an hour before taking a bath and preparing for dinner. Having skipped lunch, she was ravenous when she sat down at the table.

"How was your day today, Beauty?" Beast asked as he sat down across the table from her. "I trust you are more rested than last evening."

"Yes, I am. And hungrier, too!" She was still in the middle of the main course, and found herself examining her fingernails to see that she had gotten all of the dirt from beneath them as she reached for her cup and drained it.

"I see," he laughed as he refilled her cup.

She stopped, looking suddenly distracted. "Wait a moment. How long has it been since my birthday?"

"I'm not certain."

"Would you say perhaps a month?" she asked.

"Yes, perhaps a month. Why do you ask?"

"Just wondering. Gerard's birthday is nearly a month after mine, so it must be coming up soon. Or perhaps it's already passed."

Beast scratched through his mane of fur. "Would you like to send him a gift?"

She smiled. "Oh no, that's not necessary. I'm not even sure what made me think about it. I guess I just miss him. Well, I miss all of my brothers, but Gerard most of all. Occasionally, I'll think I miss my sisters…but a quick glance at them through my mirror cures me of that." She gazed at him curiously. "Do you have any brothers or sisters?"

"No." He looked curious as he asked, "What is it like to have so many siblings?"

"It keeps you busy." She pushed her plate away at last. "My sisters of course, didn't have much use for me in the city. I never spent any time with them. And in the country they only needed me to do their work for them. But my brothers…they were different. Of course, sometimes I was just their little sister, under their feet and in their way. But they also teased me, and taught me to play games, and…."

An odd thought had just occurred to her. She tilted her head and looked at him for a moment, considering. Then, with a smile, she asked, "Beast, do you know how to play chess?"

He looked a bit dubious. "Yes."

Cecile brightened. "Will you play a game with me? Please? It won't take long, I promise. I always lose."

"Then why do you wish to play?"

"Because I enjoy it. Please?"

He smiled at her and nodded. "All right then. When you have finished dining."

"I'm finished," she said immediately.

Before she knew it, the table was cleared and a chessboard set. She gasped, but Beast shook his head softly and said, "Don't be afraid."

"I'm not." She tried to keep her hands steady as she picked up the king and queen. The queen looked exactly like her, down to the smallest detail. Impossibly, the king was the handsome man who had appeared in her dreams. "You take the first move," she said as she resolutely replaced the pieces.

They ended up playing for several hours. Cecile was right: she was not at all good at the game, but she enjoyed herself. Every time she lost,

Beast would reset the pieces and wait expectantly for her to begin again. They talked very little as they played, but their silence was a comfortable one that didn't weigh heavily on either of them. She thought about the many times she had played this game with her brothers while her father watched them, giving her hints on what to do. Despite his help, she rarely won, but she had always enjoyed the time they spent together. Now, she was with her best friend, and the game hadn't lost any of its magic, even if the face that was now across from hers was an ugly one instead of the handsome countenance of one of her brothers.

"Of course you would be marvelous at this game," Cecile laughed as Beast captured her king yet again.

"You were very good."

"Oh, I was not. I don't think losing every game could ever be called 'very good'." She tossed one of the pawns around between her hands. "But I had fun. I hadn't played since we lived in the city. My brothers taught me to play. Gerard would even let me win. He was...." She stopped herself. She had begun to think of her family in the past tense, and that bothered her. "*Is* the oldest, and I'm the youngest, and somehow that made us rather special to each other. We had the most beautiful chess set I'd ever seen. Until I saw this one."

"I'm glad you like it."

"Of course I like it. It's wonderful." She picked up a king-piece and stared at its handsome form thoughtfully, then sighed as she closed her fingers around it tightly, pressing the silver shape into her palm.

"Beauty, are you sad?" Beast asked gently, leaning slightly forward in his chair. His eyes were full of concern for her...of love for her.

"No, I'm not sad. Just pensive."

"And what were you thinking about?"

Cecile opened her hand and looked at the king-piece again. The beautiful face stared back at hers, stirring unsettling memories. "I was thinking about a dream I have been trying to forget. And I was thinking about you."

"About me?" He looked so hopeful as he asked, "Will you marry me?"

She looked up from the silver figure in her hand. "I can't, Beast. I'm sorry."

A slight sigh escaped him, but he stood up and said in a strong voice, "Good night, Beauty. Sleep well tonight."

"Beast...."

He stopped and turned to her. She held the king-piece out to him and pleaded, "Please make me understand."

He held his hand under hers and accepted the game piece. "Understanding is the one thing in this world that I cannot give you, my dear Beauty. You must get it for yourself."

Her fingers lingered over his, just barely touching him. She slowly took them away and said, "I will try."

With a sad smile, he placed a white rose into her hand, gently caressing her delicate, tapering fingers as she clutched the flower's fragile stem. "Good night, Beauty."

Chapter Fourteen

Cecile sprinkled her favorite perfume into the bath water before submerging herself. She had seen her sisters prepare for parties and balls before, but had never imagined embarking upon such a beauty regime herself. But tonight she was taking Beast to the banquet room, and she wanted everything to be perfect. She had already visited the room again, dusting everything once more and polishing the gilded trappings until they shone. Now it was time to attend to herself.

She'd brushed her hair until every last tangle was removed so it could be more easily shampooed. The tub was afloat with sponges, brushes, and soaps, and she made use of each of them, scrubbing her skin until it glowed pink. Her fingernails were cleaned and buffed to a high shine. The shampoo was combed through her hair and then rinsed out until the water ran clear.

Her sisters had always had maids to help them prepare for their grand evenings out. Cecile was beginning to understand the necessity as she wrapped her wet hair in towels and sloshed out of the tub. She sat at her dressing table and powdered her entire body, the skin still pink from the bath. After squeezing the towels around her hair, she peeled them off and combed through the damp tresses, knowing it would be a while before they were dry enough to arrange. She donned her stockings and chemise, then struggled into her corset, lacing it as tightly as she could by herself. Draped across her bed, two gowns awaited her final decision. The first was a beautiful satin dress of scarlet, which was her best color. The other was a gown of deep purple muslin. She dearly loved the scarlet satin, which emphasized her ivory skin and brought out the brown in her copper-colored hair...but deep, royal purple was Beast's favorite color, and she knew that he loved to see her in the muslin. With a resolute expression, she returned the satin to the wardrobe and began to choose accessories for the purple muslin. If she couldn't have her favorite dress, she would at least have her favorite jewels, as her pearls suited the muslin quite well.

By the time the outfit was assembled, her hair was dry enough for her to arrange. She pinned it up into an intricate mass, weaving a string of pearls into the pretty cascade of curls. With that done, she stood back and looked into the mirror.

"I hope Beast likes this," she commented to her reflection, carefully straightening the lace and pearls, and smoothing out any wrinkles she found. Her fingers trembled slightly, and she realized they were cold as well. Nerves. She ignored them.

She carried all of the food from the table in her small dining room to the enormous banquet hall. Although she knew Beast wouldn't consent to dining with her, she set a goblet at his place, hoping he would at least join her in some wine. Then, knowing that the food would stay hot until she ate it, she returned to the small room to wait for Beast to arrive.

It seemed that she was waiting forever. Did she always take so long to eat? Just as she was about to wear a groove into the floor with her pacing, she heard Beast's footsteps in the hallway.

As he entered, he cast a questioning glance around the room. "Beauty, what have you done?"

"It's a surprise," she said, practically skipping towards him in her enthusiasm. She put both of her hands into his and ordered, "Close your eyes."

"But Beauty…"

"Just do as I say."

"Where are we going?" he asked, looking a little suspicious, but keeping his hands in hers.

"That's the surprise." She tried to give him a perturbed look, but was smiling too widely for it to work. "Come on, close your eyes." Cecile squeezed his hands and tugged him forward.

He did as he was told and she carefully led him down the corridors. As they walked past the sconces, the torches in them burst into flame, illuminating the darkened hallways. Finally, they reached the large doors of the banquet hall.

"Beauty, where are we?"

"You'll see in a minute." She released one of his hands and pushed the doors open. When she led him through, the candles in the chandeliers flared up, lighting the entire room and crackling as the cobwebs burned away. She walked Beast into the middle of the floor, hardly breathing. "All right. Open your eyes."

He stepped away from her, his eyes wide with surprise as he looked around the room. "Beauty, when did you do this?"

"I've been working on it the past couple days. Are you angry?"

"Angry? Why should I be angry?" He asked, still staring at the room.

"Well, the doors were locked. I kind of…broke in."

"I forgive you," he breathed as he walked to the table and slowly placed his big hands against the polished wood.

"Thank you." She leaned in over the table, wanting to see his face. "Are you all right?"

Tears were standing in his eyes. "Why did you do all of this yourself? I would have done it for you."

"I know you would have. But I wanted to do this for *you*."

"You are amazing, my Beauty. All of that work..."

She could feel herself blush from her scalp to her toes. "I wanted to do something for you that might make you happy." *And there's more*, she thought to herself. Taking his hand, she led him to a chair. "Sit down, please."

He sat and she poured some wine into his goblet. He looked as if he was going to protest, so she said quickly, "I hope you will join me. Just for wine. It would mean so much to me."

With a resigned sigh, he nodded.

"Thank you, Beast." She sat down and ate her dinner, watching him carefully. Every so often, he would take a cautious sip of the wine, but she could tell that it was difficult for him to drink properly. His large teeth got in the way and even his hands seemed clumsy with the goblet. The sight of those careful sips taken for her benefit touched her heart and brought her close to tears.

"Do you like it?" she asked lightly when she was nearly finished with her dinner, trying to pull him into a conversation.

"I used to, a long time ago. I had almost forgotten how it tasted," he answered, staring at the silver cup. "It's quite good."

She smiled. "I'm glad you think so. Perhaps you'll join me again some evening."

He nodded reluctantly, and she knew she wouldn't push the matter any further tonight.

"Why was such a splendid room abandoned for so long?" she asked, toying with her spoon.

"There was no need for it," he answered simply.

"But it is all right with you that I cleaned it up?"

"Yes."

She stood and walked the length of the table to his chair. "Then will you do me a favor?" Her heart was pounding and she was beginning to regret having laced her corset so tightly. All of her work for the past few days had been in preparation for this moment.

"Of course I will."

"The dance floor is so lovely, it would be a shame not to use it, don't you think? Would you be willing to dance with me again?"

A strange sort of excitement transformed his ugly face. "Whatever you wish." He took her hand and they walked to the middle of the vast dance floor. There he stood looking slightly unsure of himself. "What would you like to dance?"

"Would you be willing to try a waltz with me?"

He released a deep breath and smiled. "If you are willing to show me how it's done. I've never waltzed before."

Cecile laughed. "Well, I'll have to remember how it's done, myself. I've had little opportunity to dance it since I learned the steps a long time ago. Let's see...the music we need should sound like this," and she hummed out a one-two-three count. Soon the air was filled with a lovely melody.

"That's quite good," she complimented.

Beast grinned and raised his eyebrows. "Now what?"

She was beginning to feel almost giddy as she took him by the wrist and placed his hand against the small of her back. The tremor that went through her chest as the warmth of his hand burned through her skin caught her off guard, causing her to lose her breath for a moment. "You hold me like this and...um...I'll rest this hand against your shoulder...and you hold my other hand in yours."

His long fingers nearly swallowed up her hand entirely, but his grip was quite gentle. Cecile didn't think he had breathed since his hand had first touched her back. She wasn't so sure she had been breathing, herself. "All right, now our steps follow the beat of the music. When you move forward, I move back, like this." She led him through a few counts, then switched the lead to him.

It was rather amazing how quickly he picked up the steps; how gracefully that graceless body moved. He led her around the floor effortlessly, covering nearly every tile. The pink walls with their gold trappings went by so quickly that she might have been looking at them through a kaleidoscope.

"Are you certain you've never done this before?" she asked him suspiciously after he spun her with surprising deftness.

"My dear Beauty, I've never even heard a waltz before. Am I doing that well?" he teased.

"Doing well? You're masterful."

She moved into him, closing in the space between their bodies. It was an unconscious move on her part, but Beast welcomed her, spreading his fingers along her back.

Why, Cecile thought, was this waltz so much different than those she had shared with her brothers or the men at the few parties she'd attended? They had all been handsome, and some even graceful, but none had been so...disconcerting. The warmth of Beast's hands was absolutely indescribable; she simply couldn't think. It was getting a little difficult to breathe. And yet...and yet it was so comforting. It felt absolutely splendid to be here in this room with Beast, with his arms around her, and his eyes smiling down at her.

She lost concentration on the dance as she looked at him, her very comfort in this situation beginning to make her feel uncomfortable. Beast gradually slowed as she did until they were both standing in the middle of the floor, still holding each other, but no longer dancing. The music disappeared into the air.

"Are you all right, Beauty?" he asked, concern creeping into his eyes.

"Yes," she said as she slowly disengaged herself from his arms, immediately missing their warmth. "I guess I'm just not used to dancing anymore."

"Then we should sit down." His voice was grave, and a look she didn't understand was in his eyes.

"Yes, we should." She walked back to her chair, completely confused about what had just occurred. Her heart was still pounding wildly and she could still feel the strange weight of his hand on her waist. There was a roughly gentle feel to him—like stone and rose petals, or velvet over granite—that made her breath catch in her throat. She sat down in her chair and leaned back, feeling bewildered.

"You are a very graceful dancer," Beast said to her.

"Thank you. So are you."

"Did that surprise you?" He tilted his head to one side and looked over the candle flame to her.

"Yes, actually, it did. But it was a very pleasant surprise."

They sat silent for a little while. Cecile felt as if her mouth was packed with cotton, and drained the wine from her goblet. The thought occurred to her that if she drank enough, these strange, impossible images that were flooding her mind might be stilled.

"Beauty, do you wish to dine in his room every evening now?"

"No, thank you, Beast. I think we should leave this room for special occasions." She looked down the length of the table and smiled weakly at him. "Besides, this table is so large that I can hardly see you. I like to look at you when we talk."

"Do you truly?"

"Yes, I do."

He stood and walked towards her, and she knew what was going to occur next. Her heart trembled and she closed her eyes.

"Beauty, will you marry me?"

"I can't," she whispered, her eyes still closed.

She heard him sigh, then shift as he knelt beside her.

"I thank you so much for what you have done here. It means very much to me."

"You're welcome."

"Beauty, look at me," he pleaded softly, placing his hand over hers.

She jumped at the touch and he quickly removed his hand. Cecile turned her face to him and opened her eyes. He held a rose out to her and said, "Good night, Beauty. Sleep well."

"Good night, Beast. I…"

"Yes?" he said, hope strong in his voice.

She sighed and closed her eyes again. "Thank you for the rose."

As his footsteps echoed through the room, she realized that at this moment the thought of being left alone sent a sick ache through her entire body. "Please stay," she said softly.

The footsteps stopped. "You wish me to stay?"

"I *need* you to stay. Please don't leave me."

When she heard him sit down again, she stood up and walked the length of the table, then sank to the floor next to his chair.

"Are you all right?"

"Yes," she answered, but her mouth was still dry. She couldn't imagine why it was bothering her so much. "But may I please have some of your wine?"

His eyes widened, and he slowly passed the silver cup to her, holding it for her while he watched with wonder as she drank from it. When she gave it back to him, he held it in both hands and drank all that was left as though he had been dying of thirst.

"I'm very glad that you came here with me tonight," she said to him as he placed the empty cup back on the table.

"So am I."

She straightened the pearls on her bodice and smiled up at him. "Do you like my dress tonight? I chose it especially for you."

"Yes, I like it very much. It is my favorite."

"Good. I thought that tonight I would try to be truly beautiful for you."

Beast reached down to touch a soft curl. "Oh, Beauty…"

Catching his hand, Cecile opened his long, rough fingers and rested her cheek against his open palm, absently caressing the coarse fur that covered the back of his hand. The gold rings felt very cold against her flushed skin. "Beast, just this once, would you please call me Cecile? I haven't heard anyone say it to me in so long."

He let his thumb drift over her soft skin. "You look quite lovely tonight…Cecile."

Chapter Fifteen

Cecile's dreams had become increasingly troubling. They weren't scenes or episodes as they had been in the past, but they caused her more distress. They made no sense. There were only brief images and pictures, but they evoked such feelings of fear and loneliness that she could hardly bear it. It seemed that there was always someone talking to her and she couldn't understand what was being said, as if the person were speaking backwards. She often woke from these dreams in tears, and yet unsure of what had upset her so much.

On one night there were two voices, one gentle and one rough, talking over her. The rough voice sounded harsh and angry, like a growl. The other sounded soft and sad, like a broken music box. They were arguing, but the words floated just above Cecile's consciousness. And after that night, although the dreams didn't stop, a new sensation followed them. Whenever she was on the verge of either tears or screams, a feeling of strength and warmth and love encompassed her. It was soft as velvet and smooth as satin, and wrapped her up and calmed her, always managing to chase the demons away. She would sleep until morning, feeling safe and warm.

And on each of these mornings, just before dawn, Beast would release his fierce hold of her and slip back out of the room, trembling all of the way.

On one such morning, Cecile awoke to find a new locket on her dressing table. She opened it and a small slip of paper, folded many times over, fell to her coverlet. A poem had been written in old-style, flourished letters:

I gaze at you and hope to see

Besides the beauty there to see

Your love gazing back at me

All I have I lay at your feet

I lay my own soul at your feet

All for my Beauty so sweet

I see what is inside of you

The wondrous things inside of you

Won't you look inside me, too?

Learn to know what's not there to know

It is there inside you to know
Allow your soul room to grow
If you look within your own heart
And learn to see with your dear heart
From this cold world I'll depart

A tear dropped onto the paper, smearing the ink. "Oh Beast, what are you trying to tell me? I *can't* love you. I'm sorry."

Even so, she carefully re-folded the damp paper and put it back into the locket, then placed it around her neck. She lay back into the pillows and stared at the ceiling, feeling very forlorn. The dreams always set her on edge, and there had been so many lately that she sometimes dreaded sleeping.

Later that morning she found herself in her sewing room. There wasn't any project she felt like working on, and she certainly wasn't in the mood to start anything. She sat in the comfortable chair and leaned back, looking at her dove. It cooed cheerfully at her, but she stared at it quietly, her eyes filling with tears.

"Why do I keep you here?" she asked softly as it began preening its feathers. "Because you're pretty? Because I feel better when I talk to you? Because I need something to talk to? I've never once stopped to think how you must feel in that cage. It's a pretty cage, but a cage nonetheless."

She walked forward, placing her fingers against the thin gold bars. "Are you lonely? Do you resent me for keeping you here?"

The dove ruffled its feathers. Cecile sighed and opened the cage door. When the bird hopped onto her fingers, she carried it to the window. Pushing the glass open, she held her hand outside. After a pause, the dove flew off and circled through the air.

She smiled through her tears. "Enjoy your freedom, little one."

Her hand was already on the door when she heard the sound of wings. She turned to see the dove flying back into the room. It perched atop its cage and looked at her, blinking its serious black eyes.

"What are you doing back here?" she asked, surprised to see it. In one fluid movement, it was back within its cage, preening once more.

"So, you like it here that much?" She smiled, wondering if she would return to her cage as well.

That evening, Beast walked in wearing a smile that immediately began to cheer her. He sat down and took a deep breath, then started telling her the most ridiculous story she had ever heard. And he didn't stop with one, although she was already laughing. He continued with outrageous tales featuring the animals in his parks as though they were people with households, employers, arrogance, and impudence. When he ended with a story concerning a war between the chipmunks and the deer—in which the chipmunks built catapults to heave acorns at the King Buck—Cecile's cheeks were aching from smiling.

She brushed her hair out of her face, flushed with laughter. "Oh Beast, you can be so funny sometimes."

"Yes, sometimes."

"If I had known tonight was the night for comedy, I would have brought in some of my recent paintings. They would have given you quite a chuckle."

"But you do so well," Beast offered.

She shook her head. "It's kind of you to say so, but it's obvious that you haven't taken a look at any of my attempts."

"But I have, Beauty. I try to take notice of everything you do."

Cecile shifted in her chair. "Why?"

"To see that you are happy. And when you are not happy, I try to change that as best I can."

"And that is why you told me amusing stories this evening?"

He nodded, his eyes serious. "Yes. You seemed to need some 'cheering up', as they say."

She took a deep breath and looked around. She did feel better, as if laughter was all that she needed. Beast was observing her closely, so she smiled for him, giving him proof of his achievement. "Thank you for the stories, Beast."

"I'm glad you liked them. If they hadn't made you laugh, I was going to have to try my hand at juggling, and that would have been a disaster."

Cecile giggled. "I'm sorry for being so listless these past few days."

"Has something been upsetting you?"

With a shrug, she answered, "Just bad dreams, I guess. I used to be able to make my nightmares go away, and it upsets me that I can't do anything about these."

Beast looked at her curiously. "You can make your nightmares 'go away'?"

"Yes, some of them."

"How do you manage that?"

"My mother…she once told me something that has always helped put a stop to my nightmares."

He folded his hands and tilted his head, waiting. "Please, if you don't mind, tell me this story. I would love to hear it."

Cecile took a deep breath. "Well, my mother died when I was very young, as you know. There is so little I remember about her. We were almost never allowed to see her; she was always in her room. But when I was perhaps four years old, I was bothering my brother Victor about something or other, and to get back at me he told me that there was a monster in my wardrobe. Oh, he gave quite a description: fangs and slime and claws, and a mouth big enough he could swallow me whole. And the monster was just waiting for me to go to bed so it could eat me. Of course I was terrified, but I wouldn't show it. Until that night when I went to sleep..I dreamed about that monster in all its glory, and with the vivid imagination of a four-year-old. I was so upset and crying so much that they actually brought me in to see my mother. When I told her about the dream, she told me I was silly to be so afraid. She said that within every horrible monster, there is something small and frightened that needs to be helped; that no matter how big and scary something might be, it was once just a little crying baby like I had been. So all I had to do was to think of the little monster inside, to think how I could help that poor little baby, and the monster would disappear."

She shrugged, looking a little embarrassed. "It's remarkably simple, I know…but it has always seemed to help."

"Your mother was a very wise woman," Beast said to her in a soft voice.

"I suppose she was. I wish I could have known her. I've always been jealous of my sisters and my two oldest brothers, that they have such strong memories of her. And I've often wondered what it must have been like for her, when she knew that she was dying, to know too that Edmond and I would probably not remember her. Beyond that one memory of her, in my mind she is merely a pale face in the window, waving to me as I played in the garden, and a beautiful painting in the family gallery."

"It is still one beautiful memory," Beast said gently, "and a helpful one at that."

She was beginning to feel melancholy again, so she took a deep breath and smiled. "But when I was four her baby monster story didn't quite calm all of my fears, so she made Victor stand guard at my bedroom door until I fell asleep every night for a week!"

Beast laughed with her. "It sounds as if he deserved it."

"Yes. He was always a little more careful when tormenting me after that." She gazed at Beast, feeling more complete than she had in quite some time. "Well, now that I'm feeling better, I think tomorrow I will go to the North gardens."

"Do you like those gardens in particular?"

"It's actually been a while since I walked through them. But I remember all of the wonderful flowers that grow there. Did you plant them?"

"No. I planted nothing. They were here and have been here for a very long time. Even longer than I have. I don't know who began them."

"Well, they are very pretty, and almost as intriguing as the labyrinth in the locked garden. I like the daisies there better than almost every other flower in the gardens."

"But I thought the roses were your favorite."

"I love the roses you give me, Beast. But there are other things of beauty in your world."

He looked deeply into her eyes and said in a low, full voice, "Yes, there are things of unimaginable beauty."

Cecile's throat went dry. "Do you have any other amusing stories for me?" she asked quickly, feeling herself blush under his gaze.

"Not tonight. I am not clever enough to be amusing on request."

She gave him a look of sheer consternation and shook her head. "Don't speak that way about yourself, Beast. You are the most interesting person I know—far more interesting than the fools who used to stand up at dinner parties and gatherings to try to impress all of the young women with their silly prattling. I enjoy your company very much. I would not trade you for any self-proclaimed 'wit', no matter what."

"Do you really think that, Beauty?"

"Of course I do, else I wouldn't have said it. You can trust *my* word too, you know."

He smiled at her and hung his head. "I do not deserve you."

"No, you deserve better than me. But you have me, so do as I say and tell me another story."

He laughed and consented. "All right, another story. But I cannot promise that you'll find this one to be as much fun."

"No such morose warnings." She shook her finger at him. "You are cheering me up, remember?"

"That's right. Well then," he said with a saucy smile, "would you like to hear a very amusing story about a beautiful young woman who fell into my lily pond?"

She threw a pear at him.

Chapter Sixteen

Cecile dug furiously through her jewelry boxes. She knew that the hairpin key she'd made was in one of the boxes, but she couldn't remember which one. She finally found it hidden beneath several gold necklaces, tangled within their chains.

Feeling rather adventurous, and more than a little restless, she slipped the key into her pocket and left her room. Most of the locked rooms were found in the coldest and darkest of the corridors, so she wandered through the castle until she found it.

"Come on and open, you stupid door!" she muttered as she kicked at the fifth door on which her key wouldn't work. She gave it another kick and stalked further down the hallway.

When she was just about ready to give up and go exploring in the rain outside, one of the locks turned with her makeshift key. The creak of the door was so high and loud that it echoed in her ears for minutes afterwards. The room inside was dark and very cold and Cecile stumbled through the chamber, hearing glass crunch under her feet, until she found the window. There were no curtains, but she came in contact with some ancient and splintering wooden shutters which were closed over the window. She found the latch and pulled them open, surprised to find no glass behind them.

The sky outside brought to light the horrible wreck of a once regal room. Unlike the banquet room, which was filthy but in good condition, this chamber was falling apart. The drapes lay in rotted tatters beneath the window, and the furniture—if that was indeed what the broken scraps of wood had once been—lay in the dust which was inches thick. The glass she had heard under her feet was scattered on the floor of a long hallway which led to the room. Some of the glass was still attached to the walls of the hallway. Once there had been mirrors on those walls, but someone had shattered all of them a long time ago. Perhaps damask had once been suspended from the ceiling of the room, for strips of dirty, rotted fabric swung in the air that she had let in. The room must have been a portrait gallery, as paintings were everywhere, both hanging on the walls and scattered across the floor.

"What *happened* here?" Cecile asked aloud as she knelt in the dust to examine some broken frames. On the wall above her were the remnants of a portrait of a rather pretty woman. Near it was a painting of a small boy standing with his hunting dogs. On the floor she found a painting of an older man standing at the door to the castle.

A canvas just barely clinging to half a broken frame caught her eye, and she crawled across the dirty floor to look at it. The paint was brittle and flaking, and the canvas was in rags, but she fitted them together like pieces in a puzzle. The face that was revealed was achingly familiar. It was a portrait of the man that had appeared in her dreams.

Feeling chilled and uncomfortable at the unexpected reminder of her odd dreams, she sat up straight and turned around in the dust to leave. She gasped sharply as she looked up, for Beast was looming over her.

"What are you doing in here, Beauty?" he asked rather loudly, and she could detect a note of anger in his voice.

"Umm…just looking," she stammered, backing away from him and standing up awkwardly, brushing the dirt from her skirts.

"How did you gain entrance?"

She felt like a disobedient child as she answered, "With the key I made."

Beast held out his hand in an imperious manner and she placed the hairpins into his open palm. He put them in his pocket. "Beauty, you do not need to sneak around my castle. I've told you that you are mistress here. If something you want to see is locked, then ask and I will unlock it for you. I will do anything you ask, but this moment I ask you to do something for me."

"Yes?"

"Please, leave this chamber now and never enter it again."

She looked worried but Beast's expression was impassive. "All right," she conceded quietly.

He stood back and let her pass by, then followed her out of the room and locked the door. They walked down the dark corridor, the few sconces on the stone walls lighting as Beast passed.

"Beast?" Cecile said, for the first time in a long time unsure of herself around him.

"Yes, my Beauty, what is it?" He no longer sounded angry with her, just very tired.

"Who were the people in the portraits?"

He didn't look at her. "Those who lived here long, long ago."

"What happened to them?"

"They are ghosts now, and best left forgotten."

She knew not to question him further, and simply watched the floors as he walked her back to the main hall. There he bowed very low in front of her and said, "I will see you after dinner tonight."

Cecile captured his hand as he turned away from her. "Beast, I'm sorry I made you angry with me."

With a wan smile, he traced her jaw-line with his fingers. "I just don't want you to get hurt. The doors here are locked for a reason, and I want you to be safe. You will come to me the next time you wish to explore forbidden chambers?"

"I promise."

"Thank you, Beauty. Now perhaps you might find something in the library to amuse you for the rest of the afternoon."

She laughed softly. "All right. I suppose that will keep me out of trouble. You're not angry with me any longer, are you?"

"No, my dear."

Relieved, she hugged him tightly, catching him off-guard. "I'll see you at dinner tonight."

She felt his breath catch, and turned and left quickly, without looking back.

Chapter Seventeen

The weather was beginning to cool and the days were growing slowly shorter. Summer was dying and autumn was creeping ever so cautiously into the leaves. Although the air was rarely chilly enough to warrant a cloak, Cecile knew that the warm days would soon be a memory.

While climbing around on the garden walls one gloriously sunny afternoon, she thought about how much trouble she'd be in were she caught doing this at home. There, even as a child, she'd had to act like a 'lady'. Usually, her young heart found that to be very boring, and so she was quite often scolded. On one occasion, she and Edmond had sneaked out of the nursery with their tea cookies and proclaimed it a picnic. Cecile laughed as she thought about how much trouble that outing had caused them. She was six and he was seven, and already they were too old for 'such antics', or so their father and nurse said. That had been Cecile's last picnic, for in later years it was her sisters who went on the social outings, and she was never invited.

She stopped and sat down on the wall, thinking. Beast's grounds were the perfect setting for such an outing…and the summer was nearly over. "It would be so lonely to go on a picnic by myself," she whined before she realized that she sounded exactly like Marie. She shook her head roughly, as if to shake the whine out of her voice. "Oh well. It can't be helped."

But even as she settled on going alone, she began to wonder if there was any way to get Beast to go with her. Usually, when she wanted something, all she'd have to do is ask. This request, however, might be beyond him. He never saw her face to face in the daylight. That was a taboo which it seemed neither one of them had had courage enough to break.

"If he is in a good mood tonight, I'll ask him," she told herself as she jumped from the garden wall to the grass below.

When he entered the dining room that night with his usual salutations and a bright smile, Cecile immediately took heart. "How are you this evening, Beast?"

"I am well. And you?"

"I'm particularly well tonight. I was able to spend most of the day outside."

"Yes, I know." He folded his hands over the table. "Whenever I see you climbing on the garden walls or the statues, I always try to watch you. It worries me that you might fall and do yourself harm."

She laughed lightly at his concern. "I wish you wouldn't worry so much about me. I do all right."

"Yes, you do."

"I am glad that you watch out for me, Beast. Perhaps that's why I feel so able to do all of those things; I always know that you're there to help me should I need it."

He looked very pleased at her words and settled into the chair, watching her as she finished her dinner.

"Beast, I need you to do something for me tomorrow," she began carefully.

"Anything you ask."

"I want you to meet me here tomorrow afternoon."

He sat back, looking slightly bewildered. "I'll do what you wish…but why tomorrow afternoon?"

"It's what I want. Just come tomorrow. After my lunch."

His look was still questioning and she gave him a secretive smile. "It's a surprise…and I don't want to give you time to think about it."

He arrived in the doorway the next afternoon just as she was packing the lunch into one of the baskets that was usually used in her sewing room. She turned and motioned him inside, smiling at his tentativeness. Looking around rather awkwardly, he entered with slow, heavy steps.

"What is it you wish this afternoon?"

She placed a napkin over the food in the basket and then turned to him. "I wish to go on a picnic," she announced brightly, "and I was hoping you would join me."

"A picnic?" his voice cracked with surprise.

"Yes. The summer is dying, and I would like a picnic before it's gone." She placed her hand on his arm. "Please."

Beast looked from her to the basket and smiled. "Where do you wish to have this picnic?"

She almost laughed with relief. "Let's go to the courtyard with the large maple tree. There's always such a nice balance of shade and sun out there."

When they stepped out into the sunlight together for the first time, a slight tremor ran through both of them, and Cecile's grip on Beast's arm tightened briefly. He patted her hand reassuringly as they turned in the direction of the chosen courtyard.

Cecile found herself staring at Beast as they walked past the statues and columns of his gardens. The light glancing off of his large, curving horns offered a sharp contrast to the soft ivory warmth of lace at his throat, and the rings that adorned his huge fingers seemed out of place resting just inches beyond those deadly claws. And yet, he walked so easily beside her that she couldn't think of anyone she'd rather be with on this day. He seemed filled with some sort of unreleased tension or excitement that made his eyes brighter and his step quicker.

"I haven't been on a picnic in years," she told him, practically skipping through the grass. "What about you?"

"I don't remember ever having been, although I might have, a long time ago."

She lowered her eyes to the basket and took a deep breath, then said softly, "I've brought quite a lot of food...more than enough for two."

"It's enough for me to be here with you," he said, staring straight ahead.

Cecile tightened her fingers on the basket, determined that he would join her in lunch. She knew he would do it if she insisted, and today she was prepared to insist.

She wasn't quite sure what had come over her, but things seemed so different today. Beast seemed different out here in the sunlight, away from the shadows of the castle. And she *felt* different. She felt almost...free. How strange, that it should come to her like this. It had been many months since she'd thought of herself as a prisoner, but only today, outside with Beast in the warmth of the noonday sun, did she feel free.

While she had busied herself with setting out her picnic items on the blanket they'd placed beneath the maple tree, Beast had gotten comfortable, stretching out his long legs. He'd propped himself up with one elbow, resting his head against one large fist, the other hand on the blanket. Cecile stared at him thoughtfully while he lay there with his eyes closed. The warm sunlight, which turned her hair red, brought out a rich honey-gold color in his fur. She had never seen it look so bright. The sunlight was glinting off of his fingers in a peculiar way, and she leaned over to see why. Oddly, it was not the rings that were catching the rays, but rather Beast's long, shiny black claws. Intrigued, she reached out and gently touched one with her fingertip.

Beast's eyes flew open and he tilted his head to her, completely startled. "Why did you do that?" he asked, his voice almost a whisper.

She met his gaze, but shrugged. "Curiosity."

It was more than mere curiosity, and she knew it. But how could she explain it to Beast when she couldn't even explain it to herself.

Beast had clenched his hand into a fist at her touch, but now, his eyes never leaving her face, he hesitantly spread his long fingers against the blanket again. An invitation? A challenge, perhaps. Either way, Cecile accepted, crawling forward once more and reaching for his hand. She trailed her fingers down his, going over the large fur-covered knuckles and down to each black claw. Biting her lip, she pressed a fingertip against one shiny claw until it pierced the skin, drawing a tiny drop of blood.

"Beauty!" He was aghast.

"I'm all right," she assured him, placing the injured finger in her mouth.

He drew it back out and examined it closely, looking so horrified it was almost comical. A red dot of blood welled up on the fingertip; no more damage than she might have done with her knitting needles. Confused, Beast stared up at her. "But I don't understand why."

Cecile returned the stare. "Yes, you do," she said softly.

He started to turn away from her, but she caught him by the chin and held him there. Barely breathing, Beast froze while she drifted her fingers over his cheek to his forehead, then to his horns. When she reached the horns, a shudder ran through his entire body.

"Can you feel this?" she asked, exploring each ridge and curve of the hard surface.

Beast's voice rumbled deep within his chest, "Very softly...like the whisper of a touch."

She then plunged her hands into his hair, which felt rough as a ram's coat, and Beast hummed a sigh. Unexpectedly, he dropped his head to the blanket, his eyes closed. Cecile lifted him by his horns until he looked at her once more.

"Perhaps you would like me to stop?"

Beast swallowed hard and said, "No, never. But perhaps you should stop anyway."

With a smile, she smoothed back his unruly hair and said, "All right, Beast."

He slowly sat up and folded his hands together. After a pause in which he seemed to be composing himself, he asked, "Well then...what does one do on a picnic?"

"One eats lunch," she told him as she unwrapped the meat and cheese she had put together in the dining room and placed them onto two plates.

A look of panic entered his eyes, but he said calmly, "Thank you, but I am not hungry."

Cecile handed a plate to him. "But I am requesting that you join me for lunch."

He took the food, but made no effort to eat it. "I am not designed for this," he said softly, staring at his lap.

Her own plate untouched, she sat back and asked, "What are you afraid of, Beast?"

"Beauty," his hands were gripping the plate so tightly Cecile feared it might break, "you have learned, I hope, to view me as a friend. You have learned not to be disgusted by the sight of me. I am happy for that. But while—in many things—I can behave as a true man would, I eat as an animal. And I am afraid...I am afraid that if you witness that, you will no longer be able to look at me without disgust."

She hadn't expected such a reply, and was a little stunned by it. Her heart aching for him, she said, "Oh Beast...I didn't have to learn to like you. It wasn't through practice that I came to view you as a friend. It was you yourself who overcame my prejudices. I am your friend because you are a good person. It was a scared, angry girl who looked at you and was disgusted, but I am not that girl anymore." She reached for his arm and squeezed it warmly. "So share some lunch with me...and then we'll play in this glorious sunshine."

He sighed heavily and paused, dragging out the moment for as long as he could, and Cecile knew—she *knew*—that he was waiting in the hope that she would relent. That she wouldn't make him cross this boundary in which he felt safe. There was a certain amount of guilt in this knowledge for her, but they had come so far today, and she wasn't going to step back.

Beast took the meat and cheese in one hand, but stopped for a moment longer. "Just because I do this for you now, does not mean I can do it again. I still can *not* eat dinner with you. Please understand that."

There were tears standing in his tormented eyes, and Cecile nodded slowly and assured him, "All right, just for today."

He bit into the food she had given him, keeping his hands over his mouth to shield her from the sight of his teeth. Nothing, however, could mask the sound of them grinding and snapping together as they tore through the meat. His head jerked back as he swallowed, like a wolf finishing off its prey. It was awful, but Cecile didn't turn away. He wouldn't look at her when he was finished with that mouthful, keeping his eyes downcast and his hand over his mouth.

"Do you like it?" she asked quietly, feeling a little guilty because he looked so embarrassed and ashamed of himself.

"Yes," he lowered his hands.

"Good," she said firmly as she picked up her own plate. "There's wine in the flask. Can you pour some for us?"

He looked amazed as he obediently reached for the bottle and cups. "I didn't frighten you?"

"You hardly ever frighten me anymore, Beast."

When they had eaten everything in the basket save for some cakes, Cecile stood up and held her hands out to Beast. He took them and stood beside her, walking out into the courtyard with her.

"Isn't today just perfect?" she exclaimed, looking up into the blue sky. "I love this time of year. And today seems like one of those old romantic paintings, doesn't it? We have the weather, and the tree, and the flowered scenery. All we could possibly need would be a wishing well, or maybe a swing hanging from the tree!"

He brushed his fingers over her hands, looking deep into her eyes. "Would you like that?"

"Like what?"

"A swing hanging from the tree?"

"Can you do that?" she asked.

Even as she watched, two flower-entwined ropes spiraled down from the lowest branch. Then a polished wooden seat appeared between those ropes.

She released his hands and walked slowly to the swing, touching it just to prove to herself that it was real. "Beast, this is splendid." Cecile had to laugh at it all. "You are spoiling me *rotten!*"

"Sit down and I'll give you a push."

She immediately sat and closed her fingers around the flowery ropes. Beast stood behind her and gave her one almighty push to set the swing in motion. Cecile giggled as she rose higher and higher, feeling butterflies in her stomach, and soon Beast was laughing with her.

As he stood back and let her slow down again, she closed her eyes and simply felt the soothing motion of the swing. The sunlight was warm against her skin, and her hair blew around her face with each move forward or back. She was sighing with contentment when she felt a shadow fall across her face. Opening her eyes, she saw that Beast had moved to stand in front of her, and was watching her longingly.

"You are so beautiful," he breathed, his voice barely above a whisper.

She felt herself blush and smiled shyly. "Beast, you're embarrassing me," she said as she placed her feet on the ground to stop the swing.

"Beauty, on that first evening…when you first looked at me…what did you see?"

The question surprised Cecile. "I saw a strange, horrible beast," she answered truthfully.

"And you were frightened?"

"I was terrified."

He took a deep breath. "And what do you see now?"

Twisting her fingers around the flowery ropes, she smiled and said, "I see my dear, sweet Beast, who is good and kind, and much more beautiful on the inside than I have ever known anyone to be on the outside."

Beast placed his hand against his heart. "Is that truly what you see in me?"

"Yes. Why do you doubt my word?"

"I do not doubt you, Beauty, but what you say is so wondrous that I must convince myself that you truly did say it."

"Beast, you put too much store by me."

"That is impossible, for in you I see the meaning of my existence." He walked closer to her, engulfing her with the passion of his words. "You must understand, Beauty, that there comes a time when dreams no longer dreamt come back to haunt you, and a life no longer yours begins to mock you. And it seems that all you can think is that life can linger on and on and on. And the world can weigh so heavily upon you that you feel as if you'll crack in half…and sometimes—inside yourself—you do. Before you came here, that's all there was left in me. You saved me from that, Beauty. You saved me."

Cecile just stared at her lap and shook her head slowly, then started the swing again. He was being so open. She knew she didn't deserve such praise, and when he spoke of her so highly, she feared that she was going to disappoint him.

As the swing slowed once more, she slipped off and straightened her skirts. He followed her back to their blanket and while he sat down and leaned against the tree trunk, she stopped to gather an armful of blossoms from one of the flowerbeds that dotted the landscape. When she sat down in front of him, he watched with interest as she began to twist the stems and petals together.

"What are you doing?"

"Have you ever made a flower chain?"

"No, I don't believe so."

"I got pretty good at it when I was a child," she said as her fingers worked the flowers together. "It used to keep me amused."

With a few more deft twists, she had made a colorful garland. She crawled forward and placed it on Beast's head, where it rested against his horns. Regarding him with a smile, she commented, "Perfect. You look dashing."

"I am certain I look very silly, and I insist that you join me." He didn't, however, remove the garland.

She quickly twisted another flower chain and placed it on her hair, patting it carefully. "So, do I look sophisticated?" She sat in a ridiculous pose.

"Eminently."

At that, Cecile laughed out loud. "You should be ashamed of yourself for that lie." She laid back and looked up into the clouds. "I'm not at all sophisticated."

He watched her for many moments as she lay there. The crimson gown she had chosen was very becoming and, despite the addition of the flowers and a slightly windblown look, she had arranged her hair very carefully. Her appearance now was a far cry from what it had been during her first days in the castle. And who would have thought then that they would be out here in the sunlight together: she with her eyes closed against the bright sunlight, and he leaning in close to her, breathing in her perfume.

"You are very lovely, Beauty," he told her, "even if you do not think yourself sophisticated."

She opened her eyes and looked up at him, frowning a little as she reached up and straightened the wreath of flowers over his horns. "And you give too many compliments. You've already spoiled me, and soon I'll be vain as a peacock."

"You are a sensible girl; I don't think I could spoil you."

Cecile sat up, feeling slightly uncomfortable with him leaning over her. "You're impossible."

He gave her a wicked little smile.

Reaching over him to the picnic basket, she brought out the cake and broke it in half. "Here," she said as she handed one piece to him, "this is the best cake I've ever had."

"Beauty..." He sighed in capitulation and hesitantly bit into the cake, once more holding his hands over his mouth.

She put her hands over his and forced them down to his lap, earning a look of surprise from him. "That's better."

They remained outside until just after sunset. The evening air was very cool, and as they walked back to the castle, Beast placed his blue jacket over Cecile's shoulders. The satin sheltered her from the chill and she drew it closer around herself.

"Thanks, Beast. And thank you for coming out here with me today."

"You are very welcome."

"It's too late for supper tonight; and I'm not very hungry any way," she said, looking into the picnic basket. Both of the garlands were there, slightly wilted. She hadn't seen Beast pluck one blossom and place it inside the small needlepoint depiction of a rose that he kept in his breast pocket. She picked up her crimson skirts and swirled around lightly. "Today truly was perfect, wasn't it, Beast?"

"Yes, it was perfect."

"I had such fun! I hope that we can do it again sometime."

As they neared the castle, Beast's gait seemed to tense. He took a deep breath and began, "Beauty..."

She knew what was to follow. "No," she interrupted, her joy now gone. "Please don't ask. Please."

"I must." He swallowed hard as she drew away, dropping the basket and turning her back to him.

The jacket slipped from her shoulders to the ground where it lay unheeded. "Not tonight. Don't ask it tonight."

Her voice was choked and strained and he moved so that he could see her face. She stared at him, her lips pressed tightly together and tears streaming from her pain-filled eyes. Beast moaned softly, but straightened himself and took another deep breath.

"Beauty, will you..."

But he wasn't able to finish. Cecile had turned away and dashed into the castle, crying.

Chapter Eighteen

The next morning Cecile woke with a horrible headache. The tantrum she had thrown the night before was now taking its toll.

"You are so stupid!" she scolded herself as she petulantly rubbed at her temples. She couldn't understand what had made her react so violently to Beast's proposal last night. She'd cried for half an hour about that, then cried about being so foolish, and when she realized how she must have made Beast feel, she'd cried even more.

After drinking her water, she climbed back into bed and hid beneath the quilts and comforters. Her head was pounding and she felt like a total fool.

When she finally dragged herself into her clothes and went to breakfast, she found a glass full of an unusual, dark, cool liquid. It was very sweet and soothing and she drank all that was there. Her headache gradually eased until it disappeared.

Most of the day was spent in her sewing room. She found the basket they'd used for their picnic placed neatly in one corner of the window seat. The flower wreaths were still in it, wilted and dry, but they looked immensely beautiful to her. She hung them on the latch of the window, then sat in front of the bird cage and poured her soul out to the dove inside.

"He was so sweet yesterday," she said as she sorted through the colors of her thread. "He did everything I asked of him—as always. I made flower chains, and Beast wore one for over an hour! He looked so silly...and gentle...and...and I just wanted to...." She sighed deeply and shrugged her shoulders. "Oh, I wish you could talk to me and tell me how stupid I am."

Cecile unlatched the cage door and the bird hopped out onto her fingers. It regarded her with cold but beautiful eyes, and a look that she felt was a little superior. "Not to worry. Your look says enough." She smoothed its feathers and placed it back within the gilded bars of its cage.

"I'm glad Beast gave you to me. I'd rather talk to you than to myself."

Sitting in front of one of her large tapestry racks, she stared at the blank piece of cloth stretched over it. After several minute's deliberation, she began sketching a scene from the legend of King Arthur. Even as she carefully stitched over her drawing, she couldn't help thinking about the events of the day before.

They had done so much yesterday, and she had felt so close to Beast all day. It was a good feeling. As he talked to her, telling her stories, she let her mind trip through his voice, listening to the timbre of his words even more than to their meaning. She felt safe in that voice, and in the liquid darkness of his eyes. They had been so free yesterday…perhaps that was why she had reacted to his question the way she did. It had brought them back to the reality of their situation.

But just what was the reality of their situation? Was she still his prisoner? No. This place had ceased to be a prison a long time ago. She loved it here. And she loved…her time with Beast. She loved being with him. She wished she could be with him all of the time. But she couldn't marry him.

By the time she was ready for dinner, she had completed an entire corner of her tapestry and hardly remembered doing any of it. The meal this night seemed very quiet to her. Cecile had finished her dessert and was slowly sipping at the contents of her goblet and Beast still hadn't arrived. She was afraid that she might have upset him so much that he wouldn't come. Not willing to leave just yet, she walked onto the balcony, the cool air chilling her.

The scent of the roses was especially heavy. She leaned over the balcony railing to look at the blooms of the climbing vines, surprised but happy that they hadn't begun to wither yet. After what seemed to be ages spent outside, she turned to go back to her room. Beast was standing at the glass doors of the balcony.

"I apologize for yesterday, Beauty. I didn't mean to make you cry." He looked absolutely tortured.

"That was my fault," she said quickly, so glad that he had come, and wondering how long he had stood there in silence watching her. "I don't know what came over me. You have nothing to apologize for."

He was still standing in the curtains. "I truly, truly did not mean to make you cry."

She walked toward him and held out her hand. "I'm not angry with you, Beast. Please come out here with me."

Taking her hand, he said, "It's going to rain soon."

As she looked very far out into the night sky, she could tell that it was just beginning to cloud over. "You're right. How do you always know?"

"Most animals are sensitive to changes in the weather," he said openly.

"Oh." She turned away, feeling awkward. "I always knew when it was going to rain: whenever I forgot to bring my cloak, or wore my good satin slippers."

Beast was silent.

"I thought you weren't going to come see me tonight," she said, looking at him once more.

"I didn't want to upset you again."

"Beast—"

"No...I had to come to apologize. You were so happy yesterday, and I destroyed that."

"Beast!" she said firmly. "Stop it. I *was* happy yesterday. Everything was perfect, and I have you to thank for that. So *stop* torturing yourself over one moment. Please."

He nodded.

"Thank you." She released his hand and walked back to the railing. The clouds were beginning to obscure the moon.

"What did you do today, Beauty? You stayed inside all day."

"I started work on a new tapestry and just got carried away."

"Which subject have you chosen?"

"King Arthur and Morgan le Fay."

"I would like to see it when it is finished."

"All right." She turned around and placed her hands on top of the stone railing, intending to sit on top of it. Beast anticipated her and placed his hands around her waist, lifting her to the top. Slightly disconcerted, she said, "Thanks."

She leaned over and gazed down at the castle walls, marveling at how steep they looked from this vantage point. The faltering light of the moon cast a haunting light over the castle and its grounds. Cecile wanted to spend the rest of the night staring over that wall, but she couldn't help returning her eyes to Beast.

He looked very serious as he gazed up into her eyes, his stare intensifying as the moments passed. Her heart beat rapidly, but she didn't look away from him; she couldn't. There was a plea locked in that stare—a plea that she didn't understand only because she didn't want to understand it. Cecile shook her head slowly, not exactly sure of what she was refusing. With a tired sigh, Beast dropped his head into her lap. Months ago, she wouldn't have touched even the lace on his clothing, and this night she sat with his head in her lap and his hands at her waist, and couldn't think of moving away.

The rain began to fall very lightly. Its drops glistened like diamonds on Beast's horns, and she brushed them off with her fingertips. "It's raining, Beast," she said softly.

He raised his heavy head. "Then we should go inside."

"I want to stay out a little longer. It's only rain."

"Then I will stay, too."

She smiled at him. "Thank you. I get tired of being alone all of the time."

"I know you do. I'm sorry."

"Stop apologizing." She held her hands out to him. "Help me down, please. I'm getting a little dizzy leaning over the castle like this."

He gently placed her back on her feet and as the rain began falling harder he stood over her, partially shielding her from the downpour. She could smell his wet fur—an odor that was strangely not unpleasant. Cecile rested her head against his broad chest, feeling his heartbeat through the many layers of rich clothing, and placed her arms around him. After a few moments, his arm encircled her shoulder, covering her with his cape. Then he bent his head until his lips rested against her hair…not a kiss, but as close to one as he dared.

"How often do you stand out in the rain, Beauty?"

She giggled self-consciously. "I guess it does seem a little bizarre. When we lived in the country, I used to go out and work in the rain. I think there's something in the power of it that I love."

Beast lifted her wet hair away from her face with his claws. "You are a strange girl, my Beauty."

"It keeps me young," she said with a laugh.

He held her closer for a brief moment, then said, "We should go inside. You will catch cold again if you don't."

"I guess you're right."

As they returned inside, Beast placed a warm towel around her shoulders, startling her. "Where did you…oh, never mind. Thank you."

"Beauty, will you marry me?"

She drew the towel closely around her shoulders. "I can't, Beast."

He nodded shortly, and as he held out her rose, said, "I want you to know that I am truly sorry for upsetting you last night. I never meant for that to happen. I understand why you say no. I know what I am. But I must ask you every evening. I must ask, just as you must say no. You know that I am grateful that you are here at all. Each evening that you talk to me is a wonder, and I'm thankful for every moment we spend together." He took a deep breath, cutting off his next thought. "Good night, Beauty. Sleep well."

The door closed very heavily, drowning out Cecile's whispered words, "I'm thankful too, Beast."

Chapter Nineteen

Cecile absently watched her reflection in the mirror as she brushed through her tangled hair. With a sudden pang of guilt, she realized just how long it had been since she had looked in on her family.

Sitting back, she whispered, "I wish to see my father in this mirror."

The scene that came in to view was terrible. Her father lay in bed, pale and sickly-looking. He seemed to have aged decades since she had last seen him, and tears sprang to her eyes as she touched the mirror helplessly. She looked outside, but the sun was still high…it would be hours until dinner and her time with Beast.

"I wish to see Gerard in this mirror!" she cried.

The scene changed to her brother's office. He looked weary as well. Lavinia was telling him that their father still refused to eat. It seemed that doctors had only prescribed rest, but hadn't been able to tell them anything useful. Cecile could see nothing to calm her fears. She turned away from the mirror and the scene vanished, leaving only her reflection.

"Perhaps Beast will let me go to take care of him," she whispered to herself. "He simply must let me go. I'll beg if I have to." She sat down on the edge of her bed and began to cry, feeling miserably helpless.

By dinner, she had managed to compose herself, although she couldn't eat much of anything. When Beast finally arrived with his usual greeting, she could barely control the tremor in her voice.

"Good evening, Beauty."

"Good evening, Beast." She swallowed hard, wanting to go on but not at all certain of how to go about it. This would certainly hurt him more than anything else she might do, but it had to be done.

He looked concerned as he watched her troubled face. "Is there something wrong, Beauty?"

"Yes. Something is terribly wrong, and…" At last she stared straight at him and said in as strong a voice as she could manage, "I am breaking my promise to you, Beast. I must go. Please let me go back home."

Beast's expression fell. Indeed, his whole being seemed to sink at her words. "But your home is here with me." He was desperately pleading with her.

"Home to my father and my family."

He looked as if he might collapse. "Why? Why will you leave me when you know how much I need you?"

"I don't ask this to hurt you. I don't want to hurt you. But my father needs me, too. I saw him in the mirror, and he looks so ill. He may be dying. Please let me go back to him. Just for a week. That's all I ask."

"I gave you the mirror," he said very softly.

"You have given me everything."

He bowed his head until his chin rested against his chest. She couldn't see his face, only his huge horns and thick fur. "And I can deny you nothing."

"Oh, thank you, Beast!" Her relief turned to sadness when he raised his head. The brown fur of his face was streaked with tears. "Please don't cry, Beast."

He spoke in a tone so dark that it tore through Cecile's heart. "That is what they say out in the world, isn't it…that a man does not cry? Well, I am not a man." He took a deep, tortured breath and said, as though very tired, "I am a beast. An ugly, simple, abandoned beast."

"That's not true! And I would never abandon you."

"Yet you wish to leave."

"Beast, please try to understand. My father might be dying. I love him. Just let me spend one last week with him."

He was silent, his head bowed.

"I'm sorry."

"No, I am sorry. Of course you may go."

"Thank you," she breathed.

"I can deny you nothing," he repeated, his voice hollow.

A sudden realization awakened within her, and she stared up at him with troubled eyes. "You would have let me go, wouldn't you?" she asked. She already knew the answer, but she had to hear it from him. "If I had asked earlier, even during my first few days here, you would have let me go home."

"Yes."

She dropped her gaze to her hands and heard him ask, "Do you wish you had asked during those first few days?"

It was very strange, the emotions clawing their way through her heart and mind. She wanted to be upset. She wanted to be angry. She wanted to feel cheated. But those emotions were fleeting, and would not take root. "I wonder how my life would have changed, had I asked. But no, I don't wish it."

Beast nodded slowly. "I am glad of that. Tomorrow you will wake in your father's house." He slipped a ring off of his finger and held it out to her. "Wear this. At the end of your week, turn it and say, 'I want to go back to my castle and see my Beast again' and you will be here."

Cecile took the ring. It seemed heavy and ugly, and she had to put it on her thumb in order for it to fit. Once it was in place, however, she couldn't feel its weight. "Thank you."

"Beauty, I will die without you." A tear dropped onto the table.

"Oh, Beast," she said tolerantly.

He snarled. "I do not lie, nor do I say this to flatter you!" He took several deep gasping breaths which cut through his words. "I will die without you. I will die a little more each day you are away. So please remember me, and come back when your week is over. Otherwise you will find your faithful Beast dead."

She walked around the table and knelt beside him. "I promise you that I will come back. I'll come back, and it will be as if I never left. You'll see. You are *my* Beast, and I won't ever abandon you."

A great sob rose up in him, but he clenched his teeth over it and it emerged as a low whine. "I'm afraid it is you who will have to leave tonight. I cannot find the strength to stand."

She bit her lip, feeling so horribly guilty at being the cause of his grief that she could hardly stand it. "I'm sorry. I didn't want to hurt you, Beast. You have done so much for me. I'm so sorry for doing this, but I must."

"Pack your things in the trunk you'll find in your room. You will also find a new jewelry box from which you may choose one gift for each member of your family. Will you require anything else?"

"No," she answered quietly. She stood and turned to go, but Beast called her back to him.

"Beauty, you must take your rose."

Cecile walked back and once again knelt beside him. "Thank you," she said as she took the offered flower.

"Beauty, will you—"

"Don't," she interrupted, resting her head against his knee. She could feel the muscles in his leg tense beneath the velvet breeches. "Please don't make me hurt you any more tonight. I couldn't bear it."

She felt his fingers on her hair and inhaled deeply, trembling at his gentle touch. Cecile placed her hand over his and pulled it down further to kiss his open palm. Finally raising her head, she traced a wet tear track down his shaggy cheek and managed a smile for him. "Good night, my Beast."

"Good night."

She closed the door behind her, but could hear his heart-broken weeping far down the corridor. It seemed to follow her to her room and, although she put her hands over her ears, it continued to ring in her head.

"Just one week, Beast," she whispered as she pushed the door to her room shut. "Then I'll be back. I swear."

The empty trunk that Beast had promised her was at the foot of her bed. It was a large, ornately carved chest that seemed big enough for three weeks' worth of clothing. She searched through her wardrobe for the seven dresses that would, she had to admit it to herself, be most likely to infuriate her sisters. All of her clothes were so exquisite, but there were some that were bejeweled and made of such elegant fabrics that she knew Josette and Marie would choke on their own jealousy just to see them. In the end, she chose only three such dresses, allowing the thought of her own comfort to rule the other four. After filling one of her own jewelry boxes with her favorite trinkets, she turned to the new box she'd found on her bed.

Inside the large coffer were several tiny bottles of perfume, gold necklaces, jeweled bracelets and brooches, ornaments made of jade, a wide variety of rings, and a varied collection of other interesting and beautiful items. Cecile looked through the treasure, examining each piece thoughtfully. For Lavinia she chose perfume, carefully placing the bottle in her smallest jewelry box. Her sisters would each receive a bracelet, and she selected a ring for her father, a pocket watch for Gerard, a compass for Victor, and a jeweled dagger for Edmond. She had no idea what to give her new brothers-in-law, but settled on giving each a brooch.

After packing some shoes and underclothes and a few more items she would need, she closed the lid to the trunk. It now seemed unreal to her: After all of these months, she was going home. She was going to see her family. Beast was pushed to the back of her mind as the excitement of the moment began to creep through her.

Chapter Twenty

"Cecile? Oh my God, Cecile!"

She opened her eyes and sat up sleepily. Gerard was standing over her bed, with a frightened chambermaid peering out from behind him. "Gerard?" She threw the blankets aside and jumped into his arms. "Oh my sweet brother, how I missed you!"

He hugged her to himself, almost crushing her. "However did you get here?"

Cecile glanced at the chambermaid, and Gerard sent her to wake the rest of the family. Once the girl was gone, Cecile said, "Beast has let me come home for a visit because Father is ill."

"How did you know that?"

"I'll explain everything when I have you all together. Let me get my dressing gown, then take me to Father and I'll tell you all anything you want to know." She hugged him again, kissing his cheek before disengaging from his arms.

The new house was much bigger than even their old city mansion had been, and the furnishings were exquisite. Cecile couldn't help but think that Beast's money had been put to good use. Gerard kept tight hold of her hand as he led her through the chateau, perhaps afraid that she might disappear. Victor and Edmond met them in the hallway, still in their nightshirts. She broke free from Gerard's hand and ran to them, very happy to be engulfed in a three-fold hug.

"I see it, but I don't believe it!" Victor stammered. "Is it really Cecile?"

"Yes, it's me. Oh, I'm so happy to see you!" She kissed each of them on the cheek. "Now take me to Father. I know he's been sick."

"How do you know that?" asked Edmond, confused.

"She'll tell us the whole story when we're all together," Gerard told them, "so let's get her to Father's room because I'm dying to hear it!"

Fabre was awake and looking a bit agitated until he saw Cecile come through the door. "Cecile? You've come back to us?"

She sat on the edge of the bed and hugged him. "Yes, I'm back."

"How did you ever escape?"

"I didn't escape, Father. I saw that you were sick, so Beast let me visit you. I return to him in one week."

"No!" they all exclaimed at once.

Fabre clutched at her hand. "You can't go back to that monster!"

She kissed his hand. "He's not a monster. And he's given me this week with you. So please don't argue with me about going back. Let's just spend a nice week together as a family." She looked up at Gerard. "Speaking of family—where is Lavinia?"

"Here," came a quiet voice from the doorway.

Cecile motioned for her to come in. "Please join us. You must help tell me everything that has happened since I've been away. I know that the two of you are married, and so are my sisters. I know that Father has his shipping business again, and that all of you are helping him with it. What else has happened?"

"Well, you know much more about us than we know about you," said Gerard. "Until you sent the note and the wedding presents, we didn't know what had happened."

She smiled at him. "Beast hasn't hurt me. He let me send you the gifts and the letter." Looking to Lavinia, who sat quietly within Gerard's arms, she said, "He even chose your gift. Did you like it?"

The young woman colored up to a delicate shade of pink. "Yes. It was wonderful."

"But how did you know we were getting married? How did you know Father was sick?"

"Beast gave me a mirror which shows me anything I wish to see. So I would wish to see you, and it is just like looking through a window. I was able to watch your wedding, almost as if I was really there."

Edmond looked impressed. "So you have a magic mirror?"

She grinned. "I suppose so. The whole castle is enchanted. But with my mirror I can see anything I want. I have the best seat at the opera, I can listen to the lectures, and I can see you whenever I like. Only I hadn't been watching you for a while, and yesterday I saw that Father had become ill."

"Oh, I'm just tired," said Fabre. "But you're home again, so I'm sure I'll be better soon."

"I'll see to that. I want you looking healthy again before I leave. Now Gerard, in which room was I sleeping?"

"The guest room. I'll take you back so you can get dressed."

Cecile gave her father another hug and stood up. "Thank you, my dear. My trunk should be there, and I have presents for everyone. We should send for Josette and Marie."

"Are you sure about that?" Gerard asked wryly.

"Not really…but let's risk it," she laughed.

They walked back down the hallway together, and when they reached the door of the guest room Gerard's grip on her hand tightened. "Now promise me that you won't disappear if I let you go in there alone."

She hugged him. "You're stuck with me for the week. I promise."

The trunk was indeed there in her room. She opened it and pulled out one of the jeweled dresses, wanting her family to see how well Beast cared for her. Before she could gather up her underclothes, there was a knock at the door and a young woman entered with a curtsey.

"Mam'selle," she said with a nod, "I am Lisette. Madame Lavinia thought you might have need of a lady's maid. May I help you dress?"

Cecile smiled. "I suppose this would be easier with some assistance," she said, thinking of how many times in the castle she had wished for help with her intricate gowns.

Lisette laced her corset and set her petticoats, then reached for the gown with respect and admiration. "A splendid creation, mam'selle," she said in a hushed voice.

"Thank you. It is one of the more elaborate in my wardrobe."

"One?"

Cecile nodded to her trunk with the delight of a child showing off her dolls. The maid looked inside with wide eyes. "Oh my goodness!" she breathed.

"Yes, my…benefactor…has fine taste, hasn't he?"

"He has indeed."

In very little time, she was dressed and her hair arranged flawlessly. She thanked the young woman for her help, and found Gerard waiting outside her room when the maid opened the door.

"Little Sister, you look like such a lady!" he exclaimed.

She grinned. "I *am* a lady," she said as he entered the room. "I see you're dressed, so at least I can be sure you weren't just standing outside my door this whole time."

"Yes, we are all dressed and the family is gathering in the parlor. We've sent word to Josette and Marie. And even Father is out of bed and awaiting your story."

She grew serious. "What's really wrong with him, Gerard?"

"His conscience," her brother stated simply.

"What do you mean?"

Gerard sat down with her on the chaise and sighed deeply before answering. "I think this has been coming on ever since my wedding, when you sent me that note with the presents."

"But I wanted the note to reassure all of you that I was all right."

"I know, and it did. Believe me, my mind has been much easier since then. But Father...before that, he seemed to have made up his mind that you were dead. For him, it was a terrible thing that happened—yes—but you were at peace and in heaven, and he could light a candle for you and believe that you had forgiven him. But once we knew that you were alive..." he trailed off and squeezed her hand between his. "Somehow, the thought that you were alive and in exile and fully aware of what he had done to you brought up all of the guilt he had been suppressing. Now that guilt has him worn out. He's sick with it. He feels guilty that he traded your freedom for his life; guilty that he believed you were dead."

"Oh dear," she breathed. "Then I suppose I'll have to use this week to show him that I am happy and there is nothing to forgive."

He cupped her chin in his hand and studied her face. "And are you happy?"

"Yes. I'm lonely, sometimes. The castle can feel so empty. And I do wish I could spend time with you. But beyond that, I am happy."

"Then the Beast..."

"Takes very good care of me. You have nothing to worry about, and neither does Father."

He looked as if he wanted to believe her, but wasn't quite sure he could.

"You didn't think I was dead, did you?"

"No."

She was surprised at how much that meant to her. Gerard had not given up on her.

"The morning you left, I felt sure that you were riding to your doom. I'm not ashamed to tell you that Victor, Edmond, and I sat in your room and cried like children. We even talked of ignoring Father's warning and going after you, to kill the monster. But when Father came back with all of that money…well, it just gave me hope that you would be all right. And that the Beast told Father you belonged to him just seemed a very strange thing to say if his intent was to kill you. From then on I knew that you were alive. I could only hope that you were happy."

"Oh Gerard," she hugged him, "do you have any idea how much I love you?"

He chuckled softly. "And do you have any idea how much I've missed you?"

"What did you tell everyone when you moved back to the city without me?"

"We tried to keep our story as simple as possible. We said that you had gone to live with a wealthy acquaintance in another part of the country. We used the same mysterious friend to explain our sudden reversal of fortune, too, merely saying that an investment Father had made with this person had suddenly paid off. That explanation seemed to avoid as many rumors as possible."

"Good. I like that story. So when I leave again in a week, I'll just be returning to our wealthy acquaintance."

"But you're finally home," said Gerard. "Just stay here with us."

She stood up and kissed his forehead. "I have seven days."

"But—"

She interrupted him. "Seven days, Gerard. I promised."

"All right then. Seven days." He stood with her. "Let's go to the parlor. I know everyone is anxious to see you."

She grabbed her jewelry box and followed him to the large, comfortable parlor. One of the maids brought out tea and breads, and Cecile sat happily eating breakfast until the large front door banged open and Josette entered, looking very irritated.

"Is your driver absolutely mad?" she shouted. "Do you know what he told us? He said that—" She stopped short when she realized it was Cecile on the settee.

"He isn't mad, Josette," Fabre said from his chair. "Your sister has returned."

Marie followed Josette, her mouth open in disbelief. "Cecile?"

"Yes, it's me! Beast has given me one week with my family."

"I see," said Josette, her expression frozen. She and Marie sat down next to each other.

Cecile looked at the faces of her family. "It is so good to see all of you again."

Edmond sat behind her and wrapped his arms around her. "Good to see you, too, Ceci." He gave her a smacking kiss on the cheek, causing her to giggle.

She shook him off, but reveled in the joys of having brothers again. "Let me go! I have to hand out presents."

"Oh presents!" Edmond clapped his hands and grinned at her.

She rolled her eyes, but reached for the jewelry box. Josette took it out of her hands and looked at it critically. "Jewels for Beauty," she read off of the coffer's lid, then raised an eyebrow at Cecile. "So he thinks jewelry will make you beautiful?"

Marie stifled a laugh, but Cecile took the box away from her sisters with a pleasant smile.

"No, Josette. He calls me Beauty instead of Cecile."

"He does what?"

Cecile turned to her father. "Do you remember that? When he said 'from now on you shall be called Beauty'? He meant it! He's called me Beauty ever since that night."

"How quaint," Josette mumbled.

Cecile ignored her. "I used to ask him to stop, because it made me so uncomfortable, but he wouldn't hear of it. But that's the only thing he's ever refused to do for me. He gives me everything. Everything he can. Sometimes I feel like a spoiled child."

She opened the jewelry box. "He let me pick out presents for each of you. I hope you like them." She handed out the gifts, drawing praise from everyone. Even her sisters accepted their bracelets with a 'thank you', and took their husbands' gifts gracefully. Edmond immediately pricked his finger with the dagger, just to see how sharp it was, meriting a laugh from the rest of his family.

Josette fanned herself with a throw-pillow and looked at Marie. "Sister, I feel completely overcome. I think I should get some air. Cecile, you won't mind if we take a turn around the garden, will you?"

"No, I don't mind."

The sisters walked out into the garden arm in arm. Once out of the house, Josette stormed over the grass and plants, muttering furiously.

"I don't *believe* this is happening!" Marie whined.

"It just isn't fair. Our little brat has everything handed to her, and it's not fair! The monster hardly ever even bothers her. It seems he just shows up long enough to heap jewels onto her. It's not fair."

"Well, if he calls her 'Beauty', it just proves he's as stupid as he is ugly."

Josette nodded in disgust. "Did you see that dress she's wearing? It's embroidered with diamonds. *Diamonds!*"

"And what about the jewels in her hair?"

"Yes, but notice she doesn't have any fur," Josette said with a leer, and they both laughed until their eyes watered.

Josette sobered as an intriguing thought occurred to her. "Cecile has to go back to him six days from now, right?"

"Yes, then we're rid of her once again."

"Listen—suppose we get her stay longer than she's permitted?"

Marie looked shocked. "Why would we want to do that?"

"Think about it, ninny! If she were to break her promise, the Beast would get so angry that he would send her back without a thing. Or kill her, like he was supposed to do in the beginning."

Marie considered the idea for a moment, then said, "How could we convince her to break a promise?"

She breathed an agitated sigh. "That's the difficult part. She's always been such a stiff about that sort of thing, hasn't she?"

"Maybe we could take her to some parties," Marie suggested.

"No, she's never been one for parties."

"But we never invited her to go anywhere with us."

Josette's eyes widened. "Of course!" she exclaimed, giving her sister a quick, tight hug. "Marie-Elise, you are absolutely brilliant!"

"What?" cried the startled woman.

"We'll take her everywhere with us," she explained. "We'll be her best friends. She'll be so overwhelmed that she won't even think about keeping a silly promise." She promenaded over the flowers. "We will go shopping with her, take her to parties and gatherings, go on carriage rides, introduce her to young bachelors. She won't know what to do with herself!"

"But I don't like her," Marie whined again, following her sister.

"Do you think that I do? I hate the little hypocrite! But think of the greater goal: either we'll be rid of her for good, or she'll have nothing and will envy us!"

Marie twirled one of her false curls around her finger as she thought about her sister's proposition. "Oh, all right. If you think it will work. I suppose we could take her to see the Baroness tomorrow."

"Good idea. And if the baggage makes any grand comparisons between the Baron's castle and her own, I'll kill her myself."

Chapter Twenty-One

Over the next few days, Fabre's health did improve. Cecile made certain that she was smiling and happy whenever she spoke with him, and it seemed to lift his spirits. By the second morning, he was out of bed and talking to her in the parlor when Josette and Marie stormed the house.

"We're going to the shops today, Cecile," said Marie. "It's been so long since you've been shopping, so we thought we'd take you along for a treat!"

"But I don't have any money," said Cecile, hoping for a quick way out.

"That's all right. Just come along with us. It'll be fun," Josette urged.

"Go on, Cecile," Fabre nudged her. "You'll enjoy being in the city again."

Cecile shrugged. "All right. Let me get my wrap."

They followed her to the guest room where she lifted the cloak from her trunk. Along with it tumbled out a small black satin purse. "What in the world?"

"I believe it's a purse," Josette told her.

"I know what it is. But I didn't pack this." She untied its ribbon and shook the contents out onto the bed. Several dozen gold coins spilled out. "Oh, my goodness," she exclaimed.

"Well," Josette said a little too tersely to be friendly, "you have money now."

"Yes, I suppose I do."

Cecile silently thanked Beast for his thoughtfulness even while they were apart. Her sisters took her to all of the little shops and booths that day, and then for tea they went to the Baron's castle. That evening was spent in Josette's house, where Cecile decided that she disliked her brother-in-law more than anyone she'd ever met. He and Josette truly deserved each other. He paid Cecile plenty of compliments, but none were sincere, and most were backhanded and somehow snide. There was no topic of conversation on which he did not profess to be an expert, but actually knew very little beyond his own opinions. Cecile's mind kept returning to Beast as she sat in the presence of this handsome yet revolting man. How fortunate she was to have dear, sweet Beast, and how happy she was when it finally came time for her to leave Josette's house!

The third afternoon, the women arrived to announce that they were going to a ball and how lovely it would be to have Cecile with them.

"Oh, no thanks. I think I'd just rather stay home."

"Please!" Marie whined. "It will be so nice! All of the prominent families have been invited!"

"Really, I'd rather—"

Gerard leaned over and said with a smile, "Lavinia and I have also been invited. We weren't going to attend, but I'd be happy to escort the both of you."

Cecile hugged him. "All right then. I'll go."

"What will you wear?" asked Josette pointedly.

"I've brought some suitable gowns. Don't worry."

"All right, then. We'll be here to meet you at nine."

But they arrived well before nine, entering Cecile's room as she was dressing.

"Hello, dear," Josette said brusquely as she walked toward the chaise. "We were ready a bit early tonight, and thought we'd come over and help you dress."

"Mmhmm," sighed Cecile. Her sisters were never ready early for anything, so she wondered what their true intentions were. She didn't have to wait very long. As soon as Lisette began lacing up her gown, Josette looked at her critically.

"Are you sure you want to wear that dress?"

Cecile looked down at her gown. It was her favorite scarlet satin, embroidered with pure gold thread and trimmed in lace which glittered with gold dust. "Why wouldn't I want to wear it?"

Josette wore a mask of concern. "Well, I'm afraid your Beast doesn't keep up with the latest fashions. The fabric is lovely, of course—"

"Lovely!" echoed Marie.

"But the cut is all wrong. Perhaps you should borrow something."

She studied her oldest sister's face. Although set to a look of disdain, Josette's eyes were devouring the dress, seething with envy. Cecile smiled. "I've never been much of a fashion plate, though, have I? Thanks all the same, but I think I'll wear it. Besides, I have the perfect necklace for it," she said as she opened her jewelry box. She removed the ruby necklace and showed it to her sisters.

Marie gaped, but Josette's eyes narrowed and she said stiffly, "So I see." She gathered up her skirts hastily and said, "I only meant to help. We'll wait for you in the carriage." They both walked quickly from the room.

Cecile watched herself in the mirror. She still believed the satin to be the most beautiful dress in the world. "Lisette?"

"Yes, Mam'selle?"

"Do you think my gowns are very out of fashion?"

Lisette tied off the lacing and reached for the necklace. "The gowns are not of the latest cut, to be sure. But they are quite lovely, beautifully designed, elegantly made, and they fit you perfectly. Only the most snobbish fashion maven would find fault with them. I daresay that once society sees how well you look, the local tailors will have many a request for this particular cut."

Cecile giggled at that thought. Her sisters would be mortified if she were to start a new fashion trend!

"There now, Mam'selle. You're all ready to make your grand entrance."

"Thank you, Lisette. I really appreciate all of your help."

Gerard looked shocked when she entered the room.

"What is it?" Cecile asked, taken aback.

"You're beautiful," he said as he took her hand. "I always knew you were a pretty girl, Cecile, but I was unaware of how stunning you could be!"

She blushed. "Thanks."

"Isn't she stunning, Father?"

Fabre nodded and leaned back in his chair. "Indeed she is. I think, Cecile, that you may not be rejoining your Beast. I think it's more likely that you'll find yourself a husband this week."

Her smile disappeared. "You mustn't say such things, Father." She hastily retrieved her wrap and walked to the door.

Gerard and Lavinia followed her to the carriage. "Don't be angry with him," Lavinia pleaded. "He just wants you to stay."

"I know, and I'm not angry," she sighed. "But I'm not here to find a husband, and I'm going back just as a promised I would."

"All right," said Gerard as he took her hand and helped her into the carriage. "But tonight we're going to have as much fun as we can, and we aren't going to think of you leaving us again so soon."

"As you wish," she conceded with a smile.

The carriage lurched into motion and Cecile watched through the window as the city went by. Although it was already dark, there were still people walking about. Some appeared to be working, some just strolling, some were obviously intoxicated, but at least there were people. It made her feel a little more part of society just to be among them.

She looked through the back window to see Josette's carriage following them. It was decked out in as much finery as possible, looking like a gaudy circus truck. She shook her head and sighed.

"Tacky, isn't it?" said Gerard.

"Yes, it certainly is. I don't even understand the reasoning behind such a thing."

"You can blame Edmond for it. He managed to buy the finest horses in the city. Josette's husband wanted to buy them from him, but of course Edmond refused. So Josette set about making 'the finest carriage in the city', to try to somehow diminish Edmond's horses. You can imagine how he laughs whenever that god-awful contraption draws up to the house."

"Yes I can!" she said as the carriage pulled into the chateau drive.

Music and the sound of voices and laughter could be heard even outside. Cecile was suddenly excited about the evening. This would be her first party as an adult, and even from the street it already seemed festive. The coachman helped the three of them out, and Gerard took both Cecile and Lavinia by the hand.

"I'm going to inspire such jealousy...leading the both of you in tonight," he grinned as they walked inside.

The ballroom was lit with hundreds of candles, creating a warmth that engulfed them immediately. Many couples were dancing, looking almost like crystals in a kaleidoscope as they whirled in beautiful circles across the floor. Even more people stood at the sides of the dance floor, eating, drinking, and talking. Cecile imagined that she was stepping into her favorite painting as Gerard led her down the steps to join the party.

Josette, Marie, and their husbands entered shortly thereafter. Marie's husband had quite obviously been enjoying his own brand of festivities in the carriage and was already more than a little tipsy. Marie brushed him off quickly and took Josette's hand as they rushed to catch up with Cecile.

"Cecile!" Josette cried, immediately prying her away from Gerard. "Come on, my dear. I must introduce you to all of the important people. Gerard will have you talking to tradesmen all evening."

Gerard looked irritated by the snub, but Cecile grinned at him and rolled her eyes as she was dragged away.

"Madame Duchamp, how lovely to see you!" Josette fawned. "I'm sure you don't remember her, but this is our youngest sister, Mademoiselle Cecile Fabre, in from the country."

"Madame Devereux, Madame Larouche, good of you to come." The woman kissed their cheeks, but didn't look particularly happy to see them. She scrutinized Cecile for a moment before saying, "My dear, that is the most beautiful gown I've ever seen."

"Yes," Josette said shortly, "it's just such a shame the country tailors don't keep up with today's fashions."

Before Madame Duchamp could reply, Josette said, "You must excuse us, my dear, but I see Madame Beaumont has just arrived and I simply *must* speak with her. Come along, Cecile."

The first part of the evening went exactly like that: Josette and Marie introducing her to everyone they could find, but never allowing her one word of conversation. Cecile noticed during this whirlwind that her sisters had no real friends. They were certainly popular and knew all of the right people, but none of those people appeared to enjoy their company. And for their part, the sisters would systematically tear apart the 'friends' they had been fawning over just moments before, walking away whispering such things as "Didn't she look dreadful tonight? I've never seen such sallow skin!" or "Oh, how I detest that cow! If only it wasn't socially necessary to talk to her!"

Finally, Gerard and Lavinia were able to rescue her by sending a young man to ask her to dance.

"Yes!" she practically shouted, shaking free of Josette's hold and taking the young man's hand.

He gave her a warm smile as he led her onto the dance floor. "Your brother seems to think you could use some different company."

"My bother knows me very well," she laughed. "Are you one of the 'tradesmen' my sisters warned me about?"

"Afraid so, mademoiselle. One of Gerard's colleagues, in fact."

"Oh, thank goodness!"

He laughed as he led her through the vaguely familiar dance steps. "Does that mean you've had your fill of important people tonight?"

She smiled at him. "It means I'm finally with an important person. Anyone who helps my brother is more important than a title to me."

The young man looked pleased. "I am Alain Baptiste."

"Cecile Fabre."

"Yes, I know. Gerard has often talked about you. He didn't, however, inform me that you would be visiting."

Cecile paused a moment before answering. "Ah, well, he didn't know. I decided to visit on a whim, and it seems I arrived before my letter informing them of my intent!"

The song ended at just that moment. "Lead me to Gerard rather than back to my sisters!" she pleaded quickly.

Alain grinned. "As you wish."

Josette and Marie watched as she ignored them. Marie's eyes narrowed and Josette said haughtily, "Just as well. She'll be sorry when she's sent back without a penny and her only friends are clerks and sailors."

Chapter Twenty-Two

The party lasted so late into the night that Cecile slept until noon the next day. She awoke with a smile, though, remembering the splendor of it. Alain Baptiste had been a perfect companion, and both he and Gerard had managed to steer her away from her sisters for a good deal of the time, allowing her to fully enjoy herself.

She got out of bed, dressed simply, and joined her family at the table. Gerard and Lavinia looked as worn as she felt, and Victor and Edmond were both talking very loudly, purely in an attempt to annoy.

"It's not doing any good, gentlemen," Gerard said with a smile, "no one here got drunk last night. You're not torturing any hangover but your own."

Victor yawned. "Oh, you're useless, Gerard!"

"On the contrary, he's quite useful," said Cecile. "He kept me away from our sisters longer than I thought possible!" She shrugged as she reached for a glass of water. "I can't imagine why they've been so determined to spend so much time with me. Do you think they might actually have missed me?"

Edmond handed her a letter and said, "You can ask them yourself this afternoon. They've sent word that they'll be here to see you again."

"Ugh!" she cried. "I'm tired! I just want to lounge around the house and visit with you and Father today!"

"Well then, stand your ground," said Gerard. "Tell them you're perfectly happy to see them here at home, and don't let them bully you into going out."

When the sisters arrived, she did just that, and Josette and Marie sat in the parlor with the whole family, looking bored but determined. The next morning they arrived without sending word first, and accosted Cecile as she was eating breakfast.

"Come on, Sister!" Josette said brightly. "We are going shopping! The stores have been restocked and we're out to demolish them."

"But I was going to spend the day with Father," Cecile answered.

"Nonsense! Come with us and you can buy him something nice. We'll wait for you to get dressed."

Cecile sighed, but went to her room to dress. On her way out, she stepped into her father's office, where he was sitting on the couch. Lavinia had forbidden him to work, but he still seemed more comfortable in his office than his bedroom.

"Good morning, Father."

"Good morning, my dear. You look as if you're going out."

She rolled her eyes. "Yes. My sisters are determined to take me shopping again."

He laughed softly. "Well I for one am glad to see you spending time together. You should get out as much as possible. But be back for dinner. Your brothers and I would like to spend some time with you, too."

"I'll be back as soon as I possibly can."

"Cecile!" shrieked Marie from the foyer. "Do you need any help? The carriage is waiting!"

"Coming!" She gave her father a kiss and went downstairs to join her sisters.

After climbing into the carriage, she asked her sisters, "Are these the same shops we visited the other day?"

"We might go back to one or two, but most of the day we'll be on the other side of town. As I said, the shops have been restocked, and we are always the first to buy any new thing to arrive." Marie looked smug about that little fact.

"Are you looking for anything in particular?"

"Oh anything. My husband gave me money and I'm out to spend it."

"Same here," said Josette. "No sense in hanging on to it!"

They laughed, but Cecile could barely manage a good-natured smile.

"And you, Cecile? You've hardly spent any of that money."

She shrugged her shoulders. "I don't know. I suppose I will get something for Father. There's nothing that I really need, and Beast likes so much to give me things...I'd hate to get something for myself and deny him that pleasure." She realized she was talking more to herself than to her sisters.

"Well, maybe something will catch your eye today," Josette said tersely, exchanging a look with Marie that Cecile didn't see.

The two women absolutely ravaged the poor dress shops. Hats, gloves, shoes, and gowns were all fair game, and they seemed to care more about having the most expensive item rather than the prettiest or best made. Cecile found it all very distasteful, and soon saw her way out.

"Josette, there are some shops across the street I'd like to visit. I'll meet up with you in a bit, all right?"

Josette, who was in the middle of a search for ostrich plumes, nodded shortly. "We'll see you then."

Cecile first went to the stationer to commission a new business ledger for her father, then found a men's clothier shop.

"May I help you?" asked the pleasant-looking man behind the counter. "Let me guess: you're looking for a gift?"

She smiled. "Indeed I am. Could you help me find a nice cloak?"

"Any particular material?" he asked.

Without hesitation, she answered, "Velvet."

"Ah. Your tastes run rich." He led her to the back of the store where he ducked into a large closet. "Color?"

"Purple. The deepest shade you have."

"Size?"

"As large as you have. He's very tall and very broad. I doubt you'd have anything that was too big."

After a few moments, he emerged from the closet with a large, gorgeous purple velvet cloak. He shook it out so she could see it completely. "Is this what you had in mind, miss?"

"It is absolutely perfect," she exclaimed.

"I'm afraid it's rather costly."

"Not to worry. I'm certain I have enough with me. Wrap it up, please."

Outside, the driver was loading Marie's and Josette's purchases, so she walked on out to the carriage, the cloak carefully wrapped and tucked under her arm.

"So I see you finally bought something," Josette commented as she climbed into the carriage.

"About time," said Marie.

"I commissioned something for Father, and this is a present for Beast," she said as they lurched into motion.

Josette patted Cecile's knee in a very sisterly manner and said sympathetically, "You must hate the thought of going back to that horrid creature."

"Don't talk that way about him," she said a little too quickly.

"Why? You mean he isn't as ugly as Father says?"

"Oh, he's worse than Father's description of him was," she answered honestly.

"Worse? Truly?" Marie asked with real interest.

She nodded slowly. "Yes. Much worse. When I first saw him, I thought he was absolutely hideous. But I've gotten used to his appearance. I hardly even notice it anymore."

"That's impossible," Josette said shortly.

"No, it isn't. At first, I would just look into his eyes. He has beautiful, deep brown eyes. His voice is lovely, too. It's very rough, like the rest of him, but deep and full, and sometimes even gentle. And he is good and kind, which makes his appearance so much less important."

Her sisters gave her a very concerned look, then exchanged another of their secret glances.

"Well, if I were you, I wouldn't go back, no matter how many things he gave me," said Josette, and Marie quickly echoed her.

"I have to go back. I promised."

They finally arrived back at the house and Cecile thanked them for a pleasant afternoon before going in. Watching her with a sneer, Josette shook her head. "I don't know how much longer I can pretend to like her."

"I hate her so much!" Marie whined. "I wanted to strangle her when she talked about the monster giving her presents. As if she deserves anything."

Josette was just about to call to the driver when one of Victor's large dogs bounded up to the carriage. Instead, she nudged her sister and said, "Why, Marie-Elise, I do believe it is the Beast himself!"

"Cecile will be so happy to see him!" Marie fawned, picking up on the joke.

Josette leaned out of the carriage to scratch the big dog's floppy ears. "Look at those beautiful deep brown eyes!" she exclaimed. "Perhaps he'll bark so we can hear the lovely voice!"

They laughed so hard they could scarcely close the carriage door.

Oblivious to the scene outside, Cecile was greeting the rest of her family. She checked in on the cook to see when dinner would be ready, then went to her father's office and looked in. "You see I'm home for dinner, which will be ready in half an hour."

"Good girl! Did you enjoy yourself?"

"I suppose. I bought you a gift, but it won't be ready until next week. Don't forget to send someone for it."

"You could pick it up yourself next week."

She ignored that hint.

"Did you buy something for yourself as well?"

"No, this is a present for Beast."

He looked alarmed as she tore open the paper and held the cloak out for him to see. "You are really going back to him? I must say I don't understand why you would return to a monster now that you are back with your family."

"He's not a monster, and I wish you all would stop calling him one." She placed the cloak back into the paper, rubbing her fingers against the familiar velvet before folding the wrapper back over it. "Beast is my friend, and he's allowed me to spend this week with you, despite the pain it's causing him. I promised him I'd return, and so I'll return. I don't want to argue anymore about it." She looked at him earnestly. "It should please you to know that I am happy."

He nodded. "It does. It does."

"Good. Then let me put this present in my trunk, and we'll go down to dinner."

Dinner with her family seemed a very raucous affair after so many nights at her solitary table in Beast's castle. Stories of the day's events were told, and with as much embellishment as possible. Her brothers were the worst—telling off-color jokes and having grandiose philosophical discussions over the absolutely ridiculous. Cecile noticed that while Lavinia laughed with the rest of them, she rarely ever spoke.

She had begun to wonder if the woman ever spoke when, the next evening, as Cecile entered the small room that was her family's library, she was surprised to find Lavinia there before her. "Oh hello. I didn't expect anyone else to be here."

The young woman curled up in her chair and with a shy smile, said "Hi Cecile."

"Where is Gerard?"

"In a tournament with your brothers. They're playing cards in the drawing room."

"Cards?" Cecile said with a wry smile. "That card game they invented when they were children?"

She nodded.

"You know, when I was little, I used to watch them to try to learn how to play, but I think that every time they knew I was watching, they would change the rules," she laughed as she scanned the books on the shelf, which seemed pitifully few.

"I think they mean the game to be only for them, because they do their best to confuse me whenever I try to learn."

"Well, it's nice to know I'm not the only one they're leaving out." But she smiled fondly as she sat down with her book. "What are you reading?"

"Ovid's Metamorphosis."

"That's a wonderful work. I remember reading some of it when I was younger." She sighed. "I shall have to remember to have Beast read it to me when I get back. I'm sure he could do it justice."

Lavinia looked at her curiously. "The Beast reads to you?"

She nodded. "Yes, when I ask. He does almost everything I ask." She couldn't believe how much she missed him at that moment. She toyed with the ring on her thumb. It seemed very odd that she should miss Beast while she was with her family, but she did.

"Are you missing your Beast and his castle?" Lavinia asked sympathetically.

Cecile looked startled. "Yes, I am. How did you know?"

"You seemed a little sad just now. And to see all of your lovely things, and to listen to the way you talk about your Beast, it wasn't difficult to figure out. How did the two of you become such friends?"

Cecile closed her book, knowing she wasn't going to read it. "At first I was so angry with him, and so frightened by his appearance that I couldn't see beyond it. But he was so patient and sweet and thoughtful that I couldn't allow myself to stop at his looks. He is much more than his appearance, and I have known many who are nothing without theirs."

"Like Josette's husband?" Lavinia asked, raising an eyebrow.

With a laugh, Cecile said, "So you dislike him too?"

"Of course I do. We all detest him. We never even use his name. He's just 'Josette's husband'."

"Then yes, exactly like him. Beast is so much better than that, even if he is ugly."

"And he loves you?"

"Yes."

"And you love him."

It was more a statement than a question, and it left Cecile unable to respond. She shook her head slightly, but without much conviction.

"I hope to meet him someday. After all, in a way he is the person who brought Gerard back to the city for me."

Cecile smiled. "I would like so much for all of you to meet someday. Maybe…maybe someday." She took a deep breath and stood up. "I'm glad we've finally had a chance to talk."

"I didn't want to take any time away from your family. Gerard and the others have missed you so much."

Cecile took the young woman's hand in hers. "Well, don't disappear completely into the background. As you know, my sisters have never been very sisterly towards me. It's nice to have a girl in the family with whom I can actually hold a conversation."

"They seem to like you enough now."

"They seem to want to spend time with me, but I don't know why. We have so little in common."

Chapter Twenty-Three

Cecile awoke to find Gerard sitting on the chaise in her room. A bit startled, she sat up and asked, "Is something wrong?

"Of course something is wrong," he sounded both sad and annoyed. "Today is your last day here."

"I know, but please don't be upset. Let's just enjoy the day together," she said as she climbed out of bed and sat beside him.

He put his arms around her. "Please don't go. Please don't leave me with only Josette and Marie as my sisters. I need this sister in my life again."

Cecile was surprised by this sudden outpouring from him. "I'm sorry, my dearest brother, but I must go back. I promised."

"Is that the only reason why? To keep a promise? If so, then I will go to the Beast and reason with him. If he is all you say he is, he will understand and let you stay here with us."

She hugged him close. "I promised, but that's not the only reason."

Gerard sighed. "That's what Lavinia said. She says to let you go and hope for the best."

"Beast needs me, Gerard. Even more than you do. You have a lovely wife, wonderful brothers, a good father, a good business, and this sister who loves you, even if it must be from afar." She kissed his cheek. "I will write to you. Beast will let me, if I ask. I'll write, I promise."

He nodded, but still looked gloomy as he left her room.

When she made her way downstairs, she found Josette and Marie waiting for her.

"Wonderful news!" shrieked Marie. "We've arranged a party for you tomorrow night!"

"I can't attend a party tomorrow!" she exclaimed. "I'm supposed to return to Beast this evening."

Josette looked confused. "I thought that was tomorrow."

"No, Josette," Cecile was exasperated, "that is today. Day seven. Today."

"But we sent out the invitations yesterday, and so many are expecting to see you! You can't be so mean as to leave us without the guest of honor!" Marie simpered.

"I don't know what to tell you."

Fabre interrupted. "Tell them you'll stay one more day and attend your party. Surely the Beast wouldn't deny you one more day with your family when he has kept you away from us for so long."

And she did stay. She attended the party and enjoyed herself more than she thought possible, although Beast's ring seemed particularly heavy. The next morning she awoke determined to return to Beast in the evening, but her sisters were there with another invitation. When she declined, Josette argued that if Cecile had truly been returning to the country she could stay another day, and that no one traveled so far for only one week's visit. The next morning her father and brothers pleaded for one more day, claiming to have spent too little time with her due to her sisters, and she relented and agreed to stay just one day longer. She kept telling herself that Beast would understand and forgive her; that he would have allowed her the extra days if she had been able to ask for them.

Out of the horrible blackness stepped the silver lady. But something was terribly wrong. Instead of silver, the woman was grey, and she seemed to be very tired. She didn't speak, but pointed to a crumpled object laying at the foot of a marble bench in the moonlight. It was Beast. All around her echoed the words, "I will die without you."

Cecile woke with a start. "Oh my God!" she almost shouted. "Ten days. I stayed away for ten days! I *did* abandon him. He is the best thing in this world, and I abandoned him!"

She jumped out of bed and began dressing as quickly as she could when she suddenly felt a sick ache through the middle of her body. Then, although she was in little more than a corset and chemise, she turned the ring around her thumb and whispered, "I want to go back to my castle and see my Beast again." She immediately fell to her bed, and when she stood back up again, she was in her room at the castle.

"Beast!" she called out, hoping against hope that he would be right outside her door.

He wasn't there. She ran down the hallway, calling for him. When she reached the dining room, her heart froze. The candles at the table had burned down to nothing, leaving the candlesticks covered in melted wax. Beast's chair had been knocked backwards onto the floor with such force that its heavy oaken back had split. At that sight, she knew he would not be found in the castle.

She ran to the front doors. In her dream, Beast had been laying in the grass, dying. She put her hands over her face and sobbed. The grounds were massive. How would she ever find him out here?

"Beast!" she called out again.

Nothing answered her. She ran out into the courtyard and called for him over and over again, but got no response. She closed her eyes and breathed deeply, trying to calm herself enough that she might think a little more clearly.

"Where could he be? Where could he be?"

She had begun to run in the direction of the maple tree where they'd had their picnic, when something made her stop. It wasn't just grass in her dream…he was in the grass at the foot of a marble bench. She turned and ran for the labyrinth instead.

The rusted gate was locked, and she pulled on it with all of her might, crying with frustration. "Beast! Are you in here?" she called out. There was no answer, but something within told her that this is where she would find him. She held her breath and began to squeeze between the iron bars, glad that she wasn't wearing the skirts and petticoats which would have made it impossible. She finally emerged on the other side, a bit rust-stained and scratched, but even more determined.

She ran blindly through the maze, screaming in frustration at each dead-end, until finally she came to the marble bench where she had slept that night that now seemed so long ago. Just as in her dream, Beast was lying at its foot in the grass, still and silent.

Cecile threw herself over him and laid her head against his chest, trying to detect a heartbeat. Her own pulse was hammering so loudly in her ears that she had to wait for her breathing to slow. "Please, Beast, you have to be all right," she begged as she pushed away layers of his royal clothing and opened his shirt. Finally, she could feel a faint heartbeat and she began to cry.

"Beast, wake up. I've come home." She sobbed the words into his chest. "Please wake up."

She sat up and took his hand, holding it to her chest. "You must wake up now, Beast. You must."

A low sigh escaped him, and he moved his head slowly. "Beauty?"

Cecile smiled with relief through her tears. "Yes. I'm back."

"Thank you. I did so want to see your face once more before I died." His voice was a shadow of its former richness.

She shook her head. "You're not going to die. Please. You mustn't leave me."

He looked away from her, removing his hand from hers. "You forgot your Beast."

"No, never. I thought about you every day. I even bought you a present. I meant so much to come back as I promised, but things just kept getting in the way and...I should never have let it happen, but I did, and I'm sorry. I'm so sorry. Forgive me, please." She placed her head on his chest once more. "If you die, then I promise I will lie down beside you and I will die, too."

"You must not do that," his voice rumbled.

Cecile raised her head. "Then you must live. Because I do not want to live without you." Very deliberately, she leaned forward and kissed his lips. "You must live to be my husband."

Beast trembled as he pulled himself up against the bench. They sat facing each other for many moments as he took several deep breaths. Finally, he asked in a slightly ragged voice, "Do you love me, Beauty? Will you marry me?"

"Yes."

At her pronunciation of that one word, the sky seemed to burst into flames. She looked up and saw that the night was filled with fireworks of every color. It was almost blinding, and Cecile covered her eyes with her hands. At last she could feel that the light had evaporated into night again, but it took several moments for her eyes to adjust. And when her sight returned, she was certain that it deceived her, for Beast had disappeared. In his place sat the beautiful man of her dreams, in clothing too big for him, staring at his hands as though he couldn't believe they were real.

Cecile jumped back with a gasp of horrible surprise. "Where is my Beast?!" she demanded.

The strange man stood and reached toward her. "Beauty, I am your Beast."

"No! You are a dream!"

"A dream?"

"Yes. You and the silver lady. You can't be my Beast...you are a dream."

He closed his eyes and breathed heavily. "So that was it. I knew she was sending you dreams, but I didn't know what they were." He held his hand out to her, but she just stared at him, frightened and bewildered.

"Please, take my hand. I will explain, I promise."

She tentatively took it and let him lead her back to the bench where they sat down together.

"The silver lady is the protector of this castle, and of my family," he explained. "I tried to make her leave you alone, but she wouldn't listen to me."

"What?" Cecile's voice cracked. "None of this makes any sense!"

"It was a spell, my Beauty. An awful, powerful spell."

"A spell?"

"I will tell you everything, my dear," he said as he smoothed her hair back away from her face. "This was my family's castle, a century ago. I was the only heir. I was selfish," he confessed, staring earnestly into her eyes. "I was vain. I was cruel. Terribly undeserving of such a magnificent castle; undeserving of the people around me; undeserving of my own appearance, which masked such ugliness inside. Eventually, the protector grew weary of me, and when she confronted me with charges of vanity and cruelty, I laughed. I dismissed her as a fool." He was squeezing her hands tightly. "But Beauty, I was the fool, and all of her charges against me were correct. And she set out to teach me a lesson with a horrible spell. I would remain here in this castle until I deserved it; until I appreciated it for all it was worth. I would know loneliness, that I might learn to value others. And to strip me of my vanity, she stripped me of my looks and turned me into a beast. Since I had never given love to anyone, I would have to earn it myself, without the handsome form that might have made it so much easier. And this spell, this powerful spell could not be broken until I truly and unselfishly loved someone, and she loved me enough to consent to marry me, despite my beastly appearance." He stroked her fingers, engulfing them in his strong, smooth hands. "I don't think the protector realized what a heavy penalty she was imposing, or how long it would take to break such a spell. That's why she sent you the dreams. She was attempting to show you what I could not tell you."

She stared at him for several long moments, taking it all in. After a deep breath, she asked quietly, "Then shall I just go back to my family now?"

He looked bewildered, and released her hands in order to stroke her cheek softly. "Why would you do that?"

Cecile was feeling very naked and self-conscious before this strange man. She crossed her arms over her chest and explained, "Well, Beast needed me. But you...you couldn't possibly need someone like me."

He reached out suddenly and crushed her to his chest, tears in his eyes. "Oh, my Beauty. My dearest darling Cecile. I love you." He held her at arms' length once more so he could look into her eyes. "Have you ever doubted that I love you?"

"You?" she asked, staring into that impossible face.

"Yes, me—Beast." He thumped his hand against his chest. "For I am Beast. I still have the same heart, the same desires. And I desire you. My heart is filled with you. I want to marry you."

At that, Cecile began to cry.

The man who sat there in place of her Beast looked concerned. "Do you no longer wish to marry me?"

"Oh that's not it at all!" she cried.

He was crushing her to his chest again. "Thank God for that," he nearly wept. "And my dear, if you need time to get acquainted with me in this form, I can wait. If there is one thing I've learned in this past century, it is patience."

Cecile slowly disengaged from him, and he knelt down on the grass in front of her as she sat back to truly look at him. He waited, on his knees, while she studied every facet of this new appearance: the broad forehead and strong chin, the full lips and even, white teeth, the brown hair falling in long curls over his strong shoulders. She reached out to touch it—so much softer than Beast's rough mane. His shirt was still open, but now revealed a smooth, broad chest, with well-formed muscles beneath the pale skin. The hands resting against his thighs now had short, pristine nails rather than Beast's deadly claws. She returned her gaze to his face. His large, deep brown eyes sparkled at her in a way that reminded her of Beast's eyes...for they were Beast's eyes. Still full of love for her, still with that longing. She was home, there, in those beautiful eyes.

"I can't very well call my husband 'Beast'," she told him.

A cry of joy escaped him and Cecile suddenly found herself caught up in his arms and lifted into the air as he swung her around.

"Then I no longer have a name," he said, holding her tightly. "Perhaps you could give me a new one."

She wrapped her arms around his neck and answered, "I'll do my best."

They remained in that pose for a very long time, and when he finally set her back on her feet, he said, "Tonight, you shall sleep in my arms. Tomorrow we will take a carriage into the city. We will gather all of your family, and go to the first church we see and demand to be married right then and there. If you are ready, that is. We can wait, if you need time."

Cecile reached up and touched his face. "I have loved Beast for so long without being able to admit it, even to myself. I don't want to waste any more time than I already have."

She smiled at him, and he took her face in his hands and leaned down to kiss her. Cecile felt her heart thrill at the touch of his lips. This was so much better than any book she'd ever read; better than any love story she'd ever heard. She put her arms around him and held him close, feeling more complete than she ever had.

"Shall we go home, my Beauty?"

"Yes, my love. Take me home."